EMBERS

KAT TURNER

CITY OWL
PRESS

EMBERS
Coven Daughters Origins, #1

CITY OWL PRESS
www.cityowlpress.com

Cover Design by MiblArt. All stock photos licensed appropriately.

Edited by Tee Tate.

For information on subsidiary rights, please contact the publisher at info@cityowlpress.com.

Print Edition ISBN: 978-1-64898-277-4

Digital Edition ISBN: 978-1-64898-278-1

Printed in the United States of America

PRAISE FOR KAT TURNER

"*Song of Virgo* is an intense and perfect combination of magic, mystery, and love!" – *Jaqueline Snowe, author of the Shut Up and Kiss Me series*

"A fledgling witch finds love with a mature rock star in the midst of occult danger in Turner's magic-heavy debut and series launch. Turner sets up a promising world that readers will be pleased to return to in subsequent installments. Paranormal fans should check this out." – *Publisher's Weekly*

"In *Blood Sugar*, readers can expect Turner's trademark snark mixed with magical and metaphysical mysteries, a well-paced plot full of unexpected twists, and two layered and complex characters winning their happily ever after." – *Janet Walden-West, author of Salt + Stilettos*

"Fantastic, vivid writing and great characters make for a fun, sexy, emotional paranormal riff! Get *Hex, Love, and Rock and Roll* as soon as you can!" – *Celia Juliano, sexy, heartfelt romance author*

"Full of witchy goodness and rock n' roll magic, Turner's *Hex, Love, and Rock & Roll* is a steamy, captivating debut. Brian Shepherd sparkles as the sensitive, swoon-worthy (and feminist!) rock legend hero, and Helen Schrader is a go-get-'em heroine I found myself cheering on every step of the way! With her unique world building, smart prose, and sizzling romance, Turner is a welcome new addition to the paranormal romance genre. I can't wait to read what she writes next!" – *Angie Hockman, author of Shipped*

"*Blood Sugar* is as sexy and thrilling as it is dark and chilling. It's perfect for people ready to dive into the Halloween season and be romanced at the same time. Also- zombie squirrel." – *E. E. Hornburg, author of The Night's Chosen*

"Absolute magic. *Hex, Love, and Rock & Roll* delivers thrilling suspense, steamy chemistry, and a sexy British front man. Anyone who's ever had a crush on a rock musician or wished on a star will fall in love with this debut." – *Mary Ann Marlowe, author of Some Kind of Magic*

ALSO BY KAT TURNER

COVEN DAUGHTES

Hex, Love, and Rock and Roll

Blood Sugar

Song of Virgo

Fallen Angel

COVEN DAUGHTERS ORIGINS

Embers

For My Readers

ONE

THOM JAMES COULDN'T PINPOINT, WITH ABSOLUTE certainty, when awareness of a void in his heart switched from minor nuisance to undeniable ache. On the latest routine morning in a long string, though, the abyss had stolen more than usual.

He pulled in a drag of cigarette smoke, the woodsy flavor more rote than satisfying as a rush of chemicals cancelled out the minty flavor of toothpaste. An exhale left his lungs in a choppy whoosh, his breath ejecting filmy gray residue. Here he was again, going through the motions.

He touched the cold glass of his hotel suite window and stared down at Nashville. Or Raleigh. Or perhaps his band had played Atlanta last night. Maybe they'd delivered their music to an arena of thirty-thousand cheering faces in Orlando or Dallas.

Didn't matter. This midsize city at morning was the same as any other: paper doll cutouts of buildings, drab redbrick and concrete tones, crumbling infrastructure. The theater of the mundane unfolded twenty stories below while he watched in a fruitless search for affect or even inspiration. A smattering of affordable cars lurched to jobs. A man wearing a backpack scurried down a sidewalk, prompting a cluster of pigeons to lift off in frantic flight.

NEARING THE END OF HIS FORTIES AND HAVING PLAYED cities like this since his teen years, Thom had seen it all.

He'd felt the previous night, yes he had, high on the usual maelstrom of lust and fame.

At night, cities were sexy, glitter-sprinkled light shows teeming with promises, spectacles tailored to cater to the appetites. Come morning, though, they were little more than blight on the landscape. Interchangeable, half-real, used.

He spied a silver arch not far off in the distance, an artistic piece of architecture curving toward the clouds amid downtown buildings that weren't quite skyscrapers. Right, they'd played St. Louis the night before. That's where he was, not that it mattered.

A cynical bark of a laugh jumped out of his lips. Hollow mornings were the price he paid for his indulgent nights. The rock star's debt always came due.

From behind him came a soft, feminine moan. The bed squeaked, and the latest woman occupying whatever he called his bed sighed. The tomb in his chest gaped wider, a mocking reminder that a well-adjusted man would feel tender emotions right about now. His stomach tightened as his head spun. He stubbed out his smoke on the windowsill, snuffing his ennui.

Water rushed from the bathroom sink. Bodily noises of teeth getting scrubbed, gargling, and spitting followed. Thom smiled sadly. If their time together had been intended to be more than one night, the sounds of her freshening up might inspire intimate anticipation.

"Hey." Her voice, thick with sleep, belied a lilt of hope that toppled dominoes of guilt and regret inside him.

He turned to where she stood. A thin, white sheet swaddled her supple form, shielding the soft breasts that he'd enjoyed to the fullest. Her full-chest tattoo peeked out from the top of the material in coy glimpses of flowers crawling through emerald networks of jungle foliage.

His gaze travelled through the artwork on her chest and up to her lips, across freckled cheeks and northward to eyes as green as fresh-cut summertime grass. An inferno of chaotic red waves blazed past her shoulders.

She was quite pretty. Beautiful even, in an unconventional way with her strong features and robust bone structure. Ultimately, though, just another groupie. Another American woman in a city he couldn't place.

He didn't even know her name.

God, she deserved so much better than an empty fuck from the lowlife likes of him.

"Hi." He slid a piece of her hair through his fingers, appreciating the silkiness as he reminded himself not to be a dick. Quality aftercare in these situations kept his reputation sterling. "Sleep well?"

"Yeah. You knocked my ass out. I think it was that second orgasm that did me in. Or maybe the third. I'm pretty sure I'll have sweet dreams of the sexy British rocker for the rest of my life." With a siren's smirk, she snagged his pack of smokes off the nightstand and lit up.

Blowing rails through her nostrils, she jutted her chin in parry. Or defiance, daring him to condescend to her. Bloody hell. This bird was a live wire like none other, crackling with white heat.

Thom tilted his head to one side. Her brazenness, a shameless quality to her, piqued his intrigue. He slipped a finger into the swell of her cleavage and loosened the fabric concealing her breasts. "What's your name?"

She blew smoke in his face, the blast making him cough and blink as his eyes burned, though she didn't resist when her sheet fell to the floor. "You're an absolute pig." A touch of levity to her true statement betrayed affection. "Luckily for you, the accent *almost* makes up for it."

"You're still here. And naked again, I might add." Beneath his unbuttoned jeans, his prick swelled. He plucked the cigarette from her mouth, laid it in the ashtray, and guided her back to bed with two firm hands pushing against the velvety slopes of her shoulders.

"Touché." She walked backward in accordance with his motions, running slender fingers through the mat of hair covering his bare chest. The redhead flopped on the bed and spread her legs, her crooked smile both vulnerable and caustic. "I have a lot of problems."

His hands were busy attacking his zipper when fresh waves of shame and disgust pummeled him. Christ, what was wrong with him, screwing women as if they were mere objects? What a scoundrel he was.

"I'm so sorry." He slashed a hand through his hair, the strands as unkempt as the rest of his life, and pulled his thick mess into a ponytail in some pitifully symbolic effort to order his chaos. "Are you hungry? I can have some room service sent up if you'd prefer discretion, but if you'd like to go out, that's fine too. Or I can call you a car if you're ready to get out of here."

Her smile spread while she appraised him with a knowing, green-eyed gaze. "You don't need to pay me with food. I'm a slut, not a whore. Nothing against whores, but judge me correctly." Though she spoke in a jesting tone, her words cut like a scalpel.

She hadn't closed her legs—gorgeous pink pussy, trimmed strip of red hair—but now Thom wasn't sure if he felt aroused, embarrassed, ashamed, or some unwholesome mix of all three. He stood there blinking like an idiot, his face hot and a nest of brown pubes sprouting through his open fly while a spotlight shone on his mortified conscience.

"You aren't either one of those." He stammered, his mouth dry. Though he meant what he said—his promiscuous arse had no right to pass judgment—the words came off forced and ridiculous. "You're a beautiful person. I wished I would have gotten to know you a little better before we ended up naked."

He meant that too. Yet some unseen force stopped him, time and again, from seeking out a deeper level of intimacy with women. It was easier to approach them as empty conquests.

Easier to forget them. Easier to keep his emotional wall high and solid.

She smacked her forehead. "A beautiful person? That's the cringiest platitude I've ever heard. Can we please fuck? I don't need to witness you thumping every branch on the way down to rock bottom."

Tension and self-consciousness flew out of him in an inexplicable gust. For all his cavorting and playing the part of boorish lout, Thom never quite felt at ease or at peace. He envied the woman on the bed, how she lay there open and free, unshaken.

"Nice metaphor." He swiped the half-burned cigarette out of the ashtray, drew down a hit, and handed the smoke to his temporary partner. "Were you an English major?" She had to be in her mid-thirties and was articulate enough to be a college grad.

Her ample chest swelled as she partook, falling when she

blew out three wobbly smoke rings. He studied the multicolor splash of ink capping her breasts and marveled at the way those inquisitive eyes of hers tracked the vapory hoops as they floated before dissipating. "I'm an English professor."

He sat next to her on the bed, and she scooted over to accommodate. Considering her cue, he trailed three kisses from her shoulder to her collarbone, seeking her scent. Floral and spicy notes mixed with her tang from below. Her exotic scent suited her perfectly, even in the stark light of day. "That's sexy. Will you read to me?"

"Why, can't you read?"

For the first time, he noticed precise details of her voice. Beneath the smokiness and snark lay a melody. She spoke like a song, her rhythm rising and falling. Thom buried his face in her neck, sampling her flesh with teasing flicks of his tongue. She whined a little pleasure noise, and with that he was stiff as a bat again. "Tell me your name. Please."

"No. It's more fun this way. Anonymous."

He urged his cock from his pants and rubbed the swollen head against the soft expanse of her outer thigh, seeking relief from the pressure building in his lower belly.

"Well, you're anonymous to me, sweetheart. I'm a famous bassist, and you know exactly who I am."

The feel of his own hot breath against her skin, the arrogant truth of his cocky words, made boiling cum swirl in his balls. Sure, he got off on his own fame, notoriety, and status. No fool would dare nominate him for sainthood.

"Your ego is out of control." She punched her hips up, and he took the cue and danced teasing fingertips down her smooth stomach. "And I actually don't know you. Right now I have the idea of you, the fantasy. Which is precisely what I want."

"Fair enough." His pulse accelerated. Blood fled his brain

and filled his engorged cock. As his eyes feasted upon his partner's inviting form, he took a moment to admire the length and girth of his impressive member, the healthy purple coloring of the swollen tip. He could not wait to feed this luscious, vexing piece of feminine excellence to his hungry beast.

But for now, her pleasure was his priority. Thom might be a cad, but at least he left his bedmates with fond memories of his skills. "What do you want me to do, love? Finger you? Eat you? Rub my dick over your clit?"

"Damn, I'm all about your dirty talk." Her thighs quivered, the musky smell of her arousal intensifying.

He played with the soft curls on her mound, kneeling between her legs to admire her swollen folds and the visible bulge of her sensitive nub. He sunk two fingers inside her, licking his lips at the first touch of pussy, a tease of what his prick wanted so bad. In smooth motions, he moved those two fingers in and out, every ounce of his being committed to holding off on the raging urge to plunge inside of her and take, take, take.

"Yeah," she said, eyes glazed and lips parted.

"You want me to use my fingers?" His rod flexed, a bead of pre-cum leaking out.

Driving women crazy with his talents made him feel like a god. The potent rush of ego beat a quick one-off any day.

"Please." She sat up, her eyelids and pale lashes hooding her eyes when her gaze fell to the piston work of his hand.

"Jesus, I can see your clit. I can see how big and full it is, ripe." He withdrew from her opening and used the two slick fingers to spread her folds, making a V through which the glistening button popped like a red candy apple.

She moaned a reply and began to pinch and rub her own stiff nipples.

"I'm going to stroke your clit now, slowly with my thumb.

I don't want you to come too fast, but you're so round and red I don't know if I'll be able to prolong your climax. Forgive me."

Another unintelligible grunt from Ms. Articulate English Professor. Christ, this was fun.

He'd circle back to this very moment every time he felt a flare of remorse about how freely he fucked around.

He brought the pad of his thumb to her target, admiring the smooth, slick feel of the bump as he stroked in a big circle. A few passes around, and her clit went into spasms. She lost control, bucking and moaning as she came apart.

Using his opposite hand, Thom slid a finger back into her, hooking his digit on her equally flush G-spot, and rubbed methodically. Her inner muscles clenched and released all around his plunges, her body's responses proof of orgasm.

With a sharp cry, she froze. Her eyes stretched wide, and her jaw dropped. "Oh fuck, I'm coming."

"You sure are." Once she was done, he grabbed his dick and stroked up and down, slowly, offering a little show. "You ready for more?"

"Hell yes."

"Ah, give me that fiery red pussy, baby." With an unbridled growl, he fell on her and plunged inside her pocket of warm, liquid heaven. She'd sworn last night that she was on the pill, and he trusted that she was telling the truth.

Firm walls molded around his cock, sucking like hungry mouths as he mindlessly thrust in and out. "Goddamn, that's some bloody good snatch." He cupped one of her large breasts, pumping hard and fast in selfish pursuit of release.

"Thanks." She wrapped her legs around his hips and dragged her trimmed nails down his back. "I take good care of it. Only the best."

A laugh, this one earnest and bereft of the poison of cynicism, sprang from his lips. A weird, bubbly sensation cavorted in Thom, unnerving but not unwelcome. He slowed his strokes and gazed deeply into his partner's pretty eyes. "Does this feel good?"

"Yes," she whispered, squeezing his shoulders. His lover smiled at him, and the bubbles in his chest and abdomen swelled larger.

He kissed the tip of her nose before resuming his work, taking care this time to angle his pelvis so the root of his shaft connected with her clit when he withdrew on the down stroke.

When she began to moan again and her walls tightened and released in time, Thom closed his eyes and savored her. Her smell, her sounds, the comforts of her softness and sex. A lump lodged in his throat, and the inside of his nose stung. He'd never made love, but perhaps his current experience of the sex act amounted to a poor man's version.

"Thom, you're so good." She fell limp.

Before he could think too much about those false words she spoke and what it would mean for them to become true, he sped his plunges to the frantic, needy pace required to bring him home.

Her eyes darkened into a dirty, sinful stare. "You're about to come. Your balls are high and tight now, huh? Full of a big load you can't wait to blow."

"You're so fucking hot I can't stand it." He clutched her tit, his skin tingling as he rushed to the end. Base, unspeakable need overcame him, the tension below his waist ratcheting to a fiendish craving.

"Come all over me."

Heat unspooled near the base of his shaft. He gaped at the spot where their bodies joined, marveling at the wonder of his prick slipping in and out, his rigid flesh coated with the glisten of her juices. The second relief tore in, he pulled out and gave three final tugs right below the ridge of the head.

Thom cried out while he splintered into shocks of ecstasy. Blank and blissed with awestruck emptiness, he gawked as thick white ropes splashed her breasts, hair, and cheek.

"Fuck." Aftershocks reverberated through his body. He rubbed his stomach and squeezed his still-stiff member until the final drops of fluid eked out and dripped onto her chest.

"Now lick it off me and feed it back into my mouth."

"Pardon?" He struggled to regulate his breathing, clobbered by the double whammy of a life-erasing orgasm and her request. No woman had ever asked *that* of him.

"You heard me."

Lost in the haze of her thrall, he obeyed, scooping up his own bittersweet semen with eager lips and tongue. When he took her mouth, he forgot all about the nasty, kinky deed and melted into their first kiss.

And what a first kiss it was.

Her effort was predictably assertive, skilled from practice, though more sensual than he would have guessed. But as their tongues stroked, played, gave, and took in a series of caresses and lazy searching, a frighteningly glorious thought sunk hooks into Thom's mind and heart.

I could get used to this.

"Oh, shit." She broke the kiss with a start and lunged for a bedside table, grimacing when she palmed her wristwatch.

"What's wrong? Are you alright?" He reached for her, overcome by an irrational worry that he'd bolloxed something up and caused her to hate him. Absurd that he cared, because if she hated him, she'd leave without a fuss.

She shook her head while bending over, her pale and naked bottom a curvaceous temptation dangling just outside his reach. Last night's clothes flew onto the bed—the red bustier, black leather miniskirt, and matching jacket she'd worn to the Chariotz of Fyre after-party where they'd met. "I missed my flight."

Her body in that outfit had turned his head hard and made his tongue wag with an unspeakable urge to have her. But by now, he ought to have been feeling profound relief when faced with her impending departure.

As his nameless lover shimmied and wiggled into her clothing, the reality of her slipping away lanced him. He glanced at his hands, then the floor. *I do not want to lose her*, Thom thought with an odd and startling clarity.

Normally, he lost interest in a woman after the two of them had had their fill of sex and laughs. Yet here he was moping like a schoolboy in puppy love when he damn well ought to be thanking the good lord above that the groupie of the day was about to bolt without tears, begging, or his insistence. "Can I help?"

"No." She took a cell phone from her purse and rang someone while sliding her pretty feet into danger heels.

"What's up, Megan?" A faint male voice spoke through the line.

Thom clenched his teeth and glowered at a random spot on the wall. Megan. The stupid bloke on the phone got to know her name, but he didn't. What had this wanker done that Thom hadn't to earn the privilege?

"I'm so sorry, Gary, but I'm gonna be late for the setup tonight. I travelled to St. Louis for a work thing, and I missed my flight out. I'm going to rent a car and jet up there right now, so if the drive goes okay, I'll be onsite in time to help with equipment."

What sort of equipment did an English professor need? If he'd conversed with her in more depth than his usual flirtatious small talk allowed for, the context would have meant something. Since he hadn't tried, though, he got to sit on the bed as a clueless outsider, cursing his thoughtlessness and stupidity.

Worse, he was nothing to her. Less than nothing. He was

a lie, a "work thing." Served him right, he supposed. She was using him just like he'd assumed that he was using her. Karma was having a right-and-proper point and laugh moment.

Megan popped open a tin of mints and tossed three in her mouth before chucking the box in her bag. "Thanks for everything, stud."

She dropped a chaste kiss to his cheek, a literal kiss-off. He actually felt himself shrink.

He caught her fingers and thought fast. "It's already noon, and the sun goes down so early this month. Please, let me arrange a flight for you." That way he'd learn of her destination, her home state.

"It's only a five-hour drive to Iowa from here. I'll be fine." Glancing at the door, she slung her purse high on her shoulder.

Iowa. Noted. Megan the English professor from Iowa. Might be able to piece a puzzle together from those scraps. College departments had directories with pictures, and with any luck, there was a syllabus floating around out there somewhere with her cell number on it. "Why the rush? Aren't most universities still closed for the holiday?"

Though he'd graduated college over two decades ago, he hadn't forgotten about the existence of a winter break.

"Oh, I'm not going home for my professor job. I have a side gig." She slipped free of his hold and made haste for the exit.

"What's that?" He laid his empty hand to rest on the mattress, clinging to the phantom sensation of her final touch.

"I'm a paranormal investigator. And just so you're aware, when we were at the party I detected a negative entity or presence near your band. I don't say this to scare you, but you may want to think about getting in contact with someone who deals in exorcisms. Thanks again for last night and this morning. Bye."

Before he could ask the first of about a hundred questions invading his confused, vaguely horrified thoughts, Megan dipped out and shut the door behind her.

TWO

IF MEGAN O'NEIL HAD A GENIE AT HER COMMAND, HER first wish would be for a few additional arms.

Number two would be a cleanup solution for her messy life, but she lacked the luxury of time to ruminate on her various foibles or how to fix them.

While one hand furiously wrung her hair dry with a ratty towel that she really needed to retire, the other scrubbed her teeth and tongue. A toothbrush whose bristles had long since been flattened did its best to wash away lingering memories of Thom James. And the evil mojo loitering near him that her demon-trapping watch had picked up.

She spit out minty foam and popped her daily contraceptive pill. Not a thing she could do to help Thom now, and with any luck the watch had completed its good magical work. Megan only targeted and trapped demons. Others were required to exorcise them.

If Thom tried to track her down, she could hook him up with an exorcist. Not that she was fishing for excuses to prolong their acquaintance. Reality check: she'd never see the man again.

After heaving a resigned sigh, she finished in the bathroom and ran to her bedroom, wincing as she kicked the previous night's party clothes out of her path. It wasn't that she regretted her hookups or was ashamed of her addiction to scoring with famous guys in bands, but she often felt hollow after coming down from that initial high. Sex addiction masked some deeper problem. A spiritual vacancy maybe, or lack of passionate purpose.

She freed a bra from her underwear drawer, eyeing her extensive collection of lingerie and costumes meant to titillate. Megan fastened the bra and shimmied into undies. Sure, she loved sex. And the high that came along with landing and bedding high-status men? Priceless.

She always used protection and got tested regularly. Still, she engaged in the practices compulsively, which couldn't be super healthy. She pulled a worn t-shirt over her head, grateful that circumstances didn't afford her the opportunity to have sex with anyone at the moment.

Besides, now was not the time to psychoanalyze herself. Not when she was already beyond late and in no position to screw up her reputation in the paranormal investigation community.

She'd already screwed up at the college where she worked, with *screw* being the operative word.

She hurried into jeans and a sweater and hastily assembled an overnight duffel bag. Megan reached for the spot on her dresser where she thought she'd put her watch, but it wasn't there. How strange. Hadn't she set it down next to her jewelry stand before she'd gotten in the shower?

The timepiece had to be around somewhere. She pawed through the condoms, makeup, and tubes of hair products littering the top of her dresser. With a grumble, she shuffled around a pair of unpaid parking tickets and her dead, potted cactus, clinging to hope that her watch would materialize.

Nope. She rubbed her temples and cussed at herself. If she'd somehow lost the treasure she inherited from her Gran, the *one* talisman that helped her order her messy supernatural gift, she'd never forgive herself.

She chewed her lip, replaying the scene in Thom's bedroom, how she'd secured the clasp beneath her fingers before leaving. The latch had never slipped before, though her watch had inexplicably ended up in odd places from time to time, as if governed by a mind and will of its own. Perhaps it followed the demonic energy attached to Thom. Or fell off somehow and landed in the bed.

A rogue jolt of happiness chemicals infiltrated her system at the memory of Thom. And his bed. The thought of the bed, and what they did on those sheets, made her wet.

But again, now was not the time for lusty reverie. Besides, she'd never see him again. *Just as well.* She picked a nail. Correction: unless she turned up at another Fyre show, she was guaranteed to never see him again. *Ugh. Enough.* No more bands, no more guys. She was on a break.

Megan threw her wallet, phone, and keys into her purse and bolted from her bedroom. The weather had begun to turn bad a few miles before she pulled into her driveway, so she yanked on a stocking cap and donned her wool scarf. She was back to reality now, an entirely different world than the flashy one she'd been a part of only a few hours ago.

A growl in her stomach detoured her to a pit stop in the kitchen, where she examined her barren fridge before grabbing a large bag of chips and an energy bar from her counter and adding the snacks to her purse. She'd order groceries tomorrow. Buy stuff to make salad.

She left but then froze her march midway to the staircase. She'd forgotten something important. Crap. The door. Thanks to the brain fog induced by her five-hour commute, she'd neglected to lock up.

She went back and took care of the issue, pausing to rub her temples. "Girl, you need to get your shit together." Some prime New Year's resolution fodder right there. But first, she had a job to do, and a job she was good at if she did say so herself.

A blast of air made her shiver as she bounded down the stairs to the vestibule. George the mailman kicked snow off his boots by stomping on the welcome mat as the front door shut.

"Howdy, Megan. Sorry I'm late with the deliveries today. Old Mrs. Rolling on Third Street insisted on talking my ear off." He spoke in his friendly Midwestern tone while brushing a white coating from his jacket sleeve. A full bag rested against his back, and his brow furrowed upon spotting her duffel. "Don't tell me you're going out."

"Yeah." She winced at the whiteout blowing steadily beyond the apartment building façade's windows. "We have a gig at the St. Stephens Orphanage we can't pass up."

George chuckled, shaking his head as he turned a key in a lock and swung open the bronze door shielding several rows of mail slots. "Who pays you guys to do these investigations anyway?" He put air quotes around investigations, as usual making zero effort to conceal his patronizing paranormal skepticism.

Megan stroked the exposed skin of her left wrist. Lucky old George managed not to get cursed with The Insight, as Gran had called the heightened ability to detect and pinpoint demonic energies beyond the veil who were close to achieving their possession goals. "Usually somebody who wants to buy plumb footage of paranormal activity and hopes to sell the proof at a profit. Often, they have a taste for fame and are horny to land their own reality show."

George narrowed his eyes while sliding envelopes into their appropriate slots. "Extraordinary claims require extraordinary evidence. If ghosts were real, some enterprising guy or gal would have proven their existence by now. I say it's all baloney."

Megan smiled thinly enough to broadcast her irritation. "I don't need you to mansplain the paranormal to me, thanks."

"Okay, geez, just trying to talk some much-needed sense into ya before you head out into that blizzard chasing after make-believe fairy tales." He put up his hands in a mock-defensive position before reaching into his sack. "Drive safe. Watch out for deer."

Her insides lurched when she accepted the short stack of mail, a light tremor causing her hand to shake. Bad news surely awaited. She'd sniffed it out already in the recent way her colleagues avoided eye contact and spoke to her in more formal, businesslike tones.

"You betcha." She stepped into the night, the wind screeching as a sheet of snow blinded her with a steady diagonal gust.

Ice crystals melted on her cheeks, stiffening her lashes as she tortured herself with a long look at her second-story bedroom window. No bailing and jumping into bed. She got in her car and fired up the ignition, sighing with relief when warm air came on after a few seconds.

She threw her mail on the passenger seat and scowled at the smattering of envelopes. She picked them up, set them back down, and picked them up again before giving herself a stern order. "Get it over with."

Shoring up her emotional fortitude, Megan flipped through letters. Bill, junk, junk, bill.

The wad of tension inside of her had teasingly begun to loosen when she reached the second to last letter. From Stillwater College, her employer. A mailed letter as opposed to a phone call or meeting. Bad, bad sign.

She inhaled deeply, hugged herself, and opened the stupid

thing. A single sheet of paper, folded into neat thirds, portended doom.

Unable to bear reading the entire short paragraph from start to finish, Megan scanned for keywords. As expected, there they were:

Unfortunately. Regret. Application. Tenure. Denied.

Her heart collapsed into a lump of coal. Black ink of despair seeped from her center to her extremities, and she reread the letter to be sure she hadn't interpreted the text wrong. But denial didn't alter reality. Her application for tenure had been denied, and her employment with Stillwater would terminate with the cessation of the spring semester in May.

At the very end, right before the department chair signed off, he thanked her for her service. A flash of red burst behind her eyes.

That fucking son of a bitch hadn't *thanked her for her service* after she'd blown him in his car or bent her ass over his desk. She clacked her twin tongue barbells against her teeth, swallowing a hot load of poisonous shame.

Megan ripped the paper into pieces and scattered them on the floor before laying her forehead in the center of the steering wheel.

Bad idea, that brief fling. He wasn't married, but the smear campaign instituted by her coworkers proved enough to take her down anyway. Her entanglement with the chair hadn't afforded her any special advantages, but academics lived to slaughter their own. These ones had jumped at the first pretense to slit a young female professor's throat.

She'd made it easy for them too, with how she kept on standing in her own way.

Particularly when she wasn't so much standing as lying on her back or kneeling.

At least the ordeal of waiting had concluded, though, and

she could say goodbye to the past and focus on the future. She put the windshield wipers on maximum overdrive, hunched forward to see better, and put the little Toyota in reverse.

Crawling along at a safe speed, she drove down the rural highway to the site.

A text dinged on her phone, but she fought the temptation to peek. Megan squinted at the road, visibility limited to broken white lines against blacktop. A pale bar appeared every three feet or so amid the fog of snow. Twenty minutes of the harrowing, slow drive, and she heaved an exhalation upon pulling into the orphanage parking lot.

A cluster of five cars sat parked in some spaces near the entrance, bathed in a yellow streetlight. The old building loomed eerily, a palatial fortress of redbrick lined with dark, barred windows. Megan nodded at the structure and donned her armor of bravery.

Ghost-hunting expeditions never got un-scary, with uncertainty heightening the fright factor. Maybe she wouldn't see a thing tonight. Maybe she'd never be the same. When courting demons, a person had to be prepared for a never-ending game of Russian roulette and plenty of jump scares.

Steps slippery and careful, she shuffled to the old storage house that had been converted into an overnight cabin for the paranormal investigation crews and their sponsors who rented out the abandoned building overnight.

"Hey, guys," she said while nudging open the steel door.

"'Sup, Megs," Greg said from his top bunk bed, where he hunched over a laptop. "Glad you made it."

Another bunk bed rested against the opposite wall, housing the other two members of the overnight crew as they played with phones. Three outdated-looking space heaters buzzed, working their hardest to combat the room's humid chill. At least, judging from the partially visible toilet and sink hidden behind a privacy screen, the minimalist digs provided basic hygiene accommodations.

"Me too." Muffled by her purse, her phone chirped three more times. Geez. Who kept texting? Who cared? More important matters were afoot. "Where are we at with prep?"

"Perfect timing, actually." Greg sat up and closed his computer, pushing his stringy, brown hair out of his face. "We went through and set up the motion detectors and night vision cameras, but we were waiting for you before we did our initial walkthrough with the EVPs and energy rods. We're a little shorthanded, but with you here I think we'll be able to cover all the floors in at least a cursory manner."

"Sounds like a plan." Megan threw her stuff on an empty bottom bunk and walked to an equipment table set up in the middle of the room. She perched a pair of night vision goggles on her forehead and armed herself with a couple of portable devices meant to detect the movements and sounds of energies not of this world.

"Ready to rock." This from Lindsay, a spunky former cheerleader who blessedly held no hard feelings toward Megan following a three-month dalliance where both women discovered they were, as suspected, bisexual. The cute blonde put on her own gear. "We should get ballsy and split up. Cover more territory."

Chris, the most daring of the crew, nodded immediately. He suited up, clicking a battery pack around his waist. "Without fail, the scariest shit happens when we split up. And scary shit on video or audio, as we know, means more money in our pockets. Who's paying us again, Gare Bear?"

Typical Chris, living for the hustle. Megan didn't blame him. Come May, her side gig would become her primary livelihood, so it behooved her to stir up maximum demonic malfeasance for the cameras to rope in rich benefactors who'd pay top dollar for frightening money shots. Anxiety spiked her pulse. Talk about tempting fate.

Gary charged up his EVP microphone, fiddling with the black box until a static hiss mellowed into a droning hum. "Anonymous." He said the word too quickly, like their contractor's anonymity bothered him.

It bothered Megan as well. A chill threaded up her spine as she checked the battery levels on her devices. "That gives me conspiracy theory vibes."

Lindsay laughed. "It should give us cash flow vibes. Right, G-Man?"

Gary shrugged one shoulder, assuming his leadership role by moving to the door and heading out. "Pretty much."

Megan caught up with him. "Any clues from the email or money app account? Heiress? Movie star? Royalty?"

"Nope. The moniker on the email is MadDogMargarita, but the IP address and everything else is hidden behind firewall after firewall. Not that I asked too many questions." Gary led the brigade of four into screeching snow, and they trekked the stone path connecting the bunk room to one of the orphanage's side entrances.

"That's a weird name," Megan yelled over the wind's wail as a punishing wall of frigidity pressed into her face and burned icy hot on her nose. "As in weirdly specific. I wonder if it's a movie reference or something."

"How about less wondering and more focus on catching the good stuff." Gary spoke in an unusually tense tone and yanked open the door to the tune of a rusty creak.

"Okay, excuse me, just curious as to the identity of our mysterious, well-heeled rainmaker. Sue me." A maw of darkness and the smell of mold and musk beckoned her into the belly of the orphanage, with Gary setting a brisk pace in front.

He tossed her a scowl. "Well, we've all heard the cliché

about curiosity and its consequences for the cat. Don't be the cat, Megs."

"Ha ha." Her lame attempt at sarcasm made her feel worse, especially when Gary didn't reply and continued walking, his back to her.

The team assembled in a circle, standing in a hallway lined with rooms. The threshold of one door was piled with long-dead flowers and a couple of teddy bears stained by water and mildew, a decayed and forgotten memorial of someone who had presumably died in that room.

Megan averted her eyes from it as fast as she could, only to come face to face with the looming porcelain statue of a nun. Of all the joints the team had investigated, this was by far the creepiest. But at least she could look forward to paying down her student loans.

Gary checked his equipment. "I agree with Lindsay's statement about splitting up. The more territory we cover, the better our chances of getting a money shot. Megan, you take the basement. Lindsay will stay here and case the boarding rooms. I'll cover the infirmary and nurse's station. Chris, you've got the third floor."

Everyone extended an arm into the space between their bodies, layering hands.

"One, two, three, go." The crew spoke in unison, releasing the pep talk by throwing their hands into the air before scattering to their respective posts.

You've got this. Megan managed to transmute fear into excitement as she switched on her night vision goggles, her world going to an initially jarring combo of blackness and saturated, bright green.

The EVP wand she held beeping in a steady rhythm, she marked a stairwell and descended a short flight of steps. Her footsteps echoed, making a chorus with her own steady breathing, until she exited the stairwell and found herself in a nondescript hallway with pipes and beams crossing the ceiling. Some doors were closed, while others hung invitingly ajar.

Tucked in her sweatshirt pocket, her phone chirped again, and as she pulled it out to set it to silent, movement stirred in her peripheral vision. A shadowy blob about the size of a baseball rolled across the floor. She replaced her phone and looked again, adjusting her eyepiece. Only stillness now.

Megan pointed her wand in the vicinity of the action, mundane electronic noises travelling through her device and squealing into her earbuds. Waving the device over walls and baseboards in hopes of more blips on the radar, she walked past doors.

A shrill, static whine hit her eardrum so sharply that she flinched. A buoyant thrill soon replaced the discomfort. A lead. Megan moved a few paces down the hall, halting when the shriek of interference petered out. She backed up three steps. The shrieking noise returned.

With a resigned gulp, she opened the nearest door. A room, empty but for an overturned easy chair and some random debris on the floor. When she entered, the sound died.

Confusion mounting, Megan returned to the hallway and moved here and there. She opened doors and went in rooms, moving forward and back until she found the place where the input wailed the loudest: a random spot in the middle of the hallway.

She moved in a three-hundred-and-sixty-degree turn. "Can you hear me?"

The pitch of the screech seemed to wobble, dipping before spiking. Deniable, but enough to spur her to follow up. "Is anyone out there? Beyond the veil?"

The response was so faint that an untrained ear would have missed the whisper beneath the interference. But

Megan's ear was highly trained, so she caught two distinct words rising to the surface of the static soup: "I am."

Her heart thumped, the entirety of her awareness and attention shrinking to the sounds coming through her earbuds. "To whom am I speaking?"

"Fire woman."

Alrighty then. Right off to the weird and intriguing races. "I'm speaking to a fire woman?"

"No."

Another possibility was that the entity was trying to get a read on her, recounting elements from her life in efforts to forge a connection. They did that now and again when sizing up targets for possession, and if she maintained her wits, she'd be okay. The creeps slithered over her skin, but she persisted. "Is this a reference to me getting fired today?"

"No."

"Who do you approach me on behalf of?" Lesser demons were required to name and exalt their masters. Satan and Beelzebub in particular had massive egos. Kind of like Thom James, but he was sexy so he could pull it off. *Not the time, girl.*

"Dark trinity."

That was a new one. "Of what?"

"Coven daughters."

"As in a coven of witches?"

"Three of six. Fire woman."

"Where are the witches?"

"Beneath you."

"What do they want?"

"Fire woman. Beneath you."

She pinched her chin. This interaction had veered well into circular territory, a bad sign that meant an entity was losing interest in communicating. There had to be a path out of the loop. "Who or what are you?"

"Prophecy. Earth, fire, chaos." The second syllable of the last word echoed with a snakelike hissing sound.

Okay. Minimal but legitimate progress.

"What's your connection to the coven daughters and the dark trinity?"

"Beneath you. Release me."

The hairs on the back of her neck stood. She was being watched. An itchy sizzle of adrenaline frying her nerves, Megan jerked her head over her shoulder. Only the empty hallway, glowing green, faced her. She sighed and returned her stare to the front.

"Prophecy comes."

"When?"

"Six."

Megan bucked up and prepped a key question that would reveal the supernatural speaker's intention once and for all. "What would you like me to do?"

"Kneel."

She sighed. "Sorry, buddy. Hard no."

Bending the knee to a demon was the express route to possession. Even though she hadn't confirmed her new pal's demonic status, she wasn't about to risk becoming some fiend's earthly vessel. She checked her digital recording device, confirming with a glimpse at the red light that it was indeed recording. Might be about time to duck out of this chat. She'd caught plenty of tangible audio and could solidly place this investigation in the win column.

The entity insisted, "Kneel not in fealty."

She tapped her foot, reluctantly drawn back into the fold. "In what, then?"

"Kneel. Search. Dig. Fire woman."

A light of insight flashed near Megan's forehead. This visitor didn't want to possess her, it wanted to guide or direct her to whatever this fire woman deal was all about.

Megan dropped to her hands and knees, crawling across the ground while waving her wand with one hand and palming the concrete flooring with the other. After a few minutes, a loose chunk wobbled beneath her hand. Blood roared in her ears while she committed to a choice both undeniably brave and perhaps stupid.

A square panel of crumbly rock gave way against her pull as she lifted the slab, revealing a gap in the floor that housed an object. She leaned forward, peering in, and identified a fat book the size of an encyclopedia.

When she lifted it, the instant she felt its heaviness in her hold and the leathery thickness of its cover, Megan's feet lifted off the ground, peeling from heels to toes. She gasped, realizing that the voice from beyond had left.

She stammered, kicking helplessly in the air as she rose in a slow float upward. Her back arched, belly curving toward the ceiling. Her arms floated to the sides in a T-shape.

The book fell from her hand and hit the floor with a thump. Pages flipped rapidly on their own volition. Terror shot through Megan in frantic streaks, intensifying when her head jerked back like someone had pulled her hair, leaving her neck exposed and vulnerable.

She opened her mouth to scream, but the cry stuck in her throat when a cloud of mist rose from the split belly of the book and floated toward her upended face.

A cloying aroma overcame her, so intoxicating that all she could do was pant and inhale rosy cinnamon sweetness.

The voice returned, blabbering with such excited speed that speech amounted to little more than gibberish. Yet as she clutched a death grip on her recording device so it wouldn't crash to the floor and break, Megan caught a cluster of breathy keywords in the nonsense:

"Fire witch. Dark trinity. Prophecy. Level one sex magic. Awaken me. Awaken me!"

She may have spoken too, words of questioning or protest, but she was too spaced out by the perfume cloud to say for sure.

She began to fade to black, upside down and out of her head from the effects of the delicious drug, when Gary's shocked voice ripped her from her stupor: "Megan, Jesus Christ!"

THREE

With an ugly crack, pain slammed into Megan's spine and shoulders as she hit the floor. She wheezed, desperate for a breath that wouldn't quite come, and rolled to a fetal position while shoving the disorienting night vision goggles off her head.

A squatting Gary faced her, aiming a digital camera in her face. "We found you floating in the arch of hysteria," he said breathlessly. "The ultimate sign of possession and human despair. Can you describe the events leading up to your levitation? Give the details of what happened?"

Nausea clamped her gut, and she gagged as a sickening headache pulsed near her temple. "It's all on the audio recording." She squeezed her eyes shut and willed away the urge to vomit. "Please get that out of my face."

"You okay, Megs?" Chris asked with concern.

"Yeah, you took a wicked hit there." Lindsay crouched to rub Megan's back.

"I guess." She pressed her palms into her eyes until her universe stopped spinning and the contents of her stomach settled. Gingerly, she opened her eyes and blinked. Blurry blobs coalesced into form. "I need to go lie down."

"Of course." Gary extended one hand and collected her discarded goggles with his other. "I cannot *wait* for all of us to watch and listen to this. You caught gold, Megan. Pure gold."

Megan accepted her teammate's grip and rolled to sit, battening down against a fresh onslaught of dizziness. Once lucid enough to stand, she collected the book and rose. "Yep. And I cannot *wait* to relive my trauma." She laid on just enough sarcasm for him to back off, and he muttered an apology.

"What's with the tome?" Lindsay asked.

"The entity I contacted guided me to it." Megan squeezed the prize to her chest while trekking upstairs with the team.

"You sure it's safe to take?" Chris jogged up the stairs.

"Nope." She ran a finger through a groove in the cover's leather, curious to dive into the text and learn about this alleged prophecy and her role. "But I'm going to anyway."

Gary laughed. "Classic Megan."

"No, classic Megan would be if she contacted a hot incubus and got it on with him." Lindsay elbowed Megan's side, her teasing playful.

"Wow, I just got owned. Top tier. Seriously," Megan said dryly, though she appreciated the good-natured levity. Lindsay was the best sort of friend when it came to cutting tension.

By the time they returned to the bunkhouse and got settled in, Megan had regained her bearings and felt well enough to spend some quality time poring over the strange volume.

Gary climbed the ladder to his top bunk. Wood creaked as he got comfortable, sound tapering to silence after several minutes.

Lindsay yawned, and Chris's sleep sounds app played a tapping rainfall pattern.

While her colleagues dozed, Chris snoring unobtrusively, Megan rummaged in her duffel for her reading light. Her arm brushed the hard edge of her cell phone through sweatshirt fabric.

Might as well check those texts.

She clicked on the message icon and checked a few uninteresting texts: a reminder from the dentist and some political solicitation. The next one in the string came from an unknown number. Upon opening the third, she sat up straighter, smiling as she read the message.

Did you make it home alright? You left your watch in the hotel.

Despite the scary ordeal that went down in the basement, the stirrings of giddy flutters flirted. He'd had to have exerted some effort to find her cell phone number. Of course, reconnecting with Thom wouldn't lead anywhere meaningful, but his inviting further communication meant that she could indulge in a little fun, harmless flirting. If for no other reason than to enjoy a temporary distraction from the earlier craziness.

She'd have plenty of time to focus on the developments later while brainstorming with the rest of the team. She needed a break.

Yeah. Thanks. I can stop by your next show and grab it.

She chewed her lip, staring at the screen. Was inviting herself to another concert too forward? Not like she had tons of options. Trusting the postal service with her prized possession certainly wasn't among them.

That's not for three days. I can bring it to you. And talk about the last thing you said before leaving. You said you live in Iowa?

Megan released a solemn breath. Fair enough. This wasn't about fun. She owed him an explanation for her cryptic comments, and his returning the watch would serve as a natural transition into a discussion of her abilities. He might balk and call her a nutcase, but that was on him.

Yes. I live in a small town called New Denmark. The closest airport is Cedar Rapids, and from there you're looking at a 45 minute drive on the interstate.

I'll be there in a few hours. What's your address?

Thom sure was giving himself an optimistic ETA, especially given the arctic conditions, but he was famous and connected. For all she knew, he owned a private jet or had a close friend who did.

She went to the door and peeked outside. Brisk wind lashed snow to the ground in relentless streaks. At least five inches had accumulated. A snowplow chugged down the highway, the vehicle's movement eerily out of place in the tranquil polar landscape.

This wasn't going to work out, unfortunately. *I'm not home, I'm staying overnight at the old St. John's Orphanage off Highway 53. Weather's nasty, though. Neither one of us should be driving.*

You stay put. Don't worry about me. See you soon, Megan.

She shook her head in preemptive concern for him. *You sure?*

Positive.

Ok. Text me if you have any issues or need directions.

He responded with a checkmark emoji, a trivial detail that gave her more pleasure than she had a right to feel. Because it made her wonder about his personality, his traits.

Was he efficient, meticulous, organized? You learned some things about a person based on how they acted in bed, though sex made for a comparatively superficial form of interaction.

Her sex life remained relegated to the emotional surface, that was. Maybe other people touched the depths of their partners' souls or whatever.

Megan drew her knees to her chest and set her phone

down, compelled by a contemplative ache beneath her ribs. Having lots of casual sex gave her a designated space in which to play extrovert while protecting her heart from those who would stomp on her tender center.

Once the third of three reckless musician boys crushed her nearly beyond recognition, she'd instituted her "no more serious relationships" policy. And her decision to partake only in superficial affairs was working out *fine*. She pulled an errant thread on her sweater as a couple of the more dignity-soiling encounters with the department chair bobbed up from their watery graves.

Ugh, what was with all the navel gazing lately? She shook thoughts out of her head and turned to her book.

After a stint of attempting to read the book cover to cover, she hadn't cracked the impenetrable contents as deeply as she'd hoped. A lot of the material was written in arcane languages foreign to her, and she lacked a frame of reference for the pages of symbols, sigils, and runes.

Megan massaged her itchy eyes with her knuckles. Perhaps she needed an interpreter, someone skilled in magic or witchcraft to help her understand this material.

The entity had mentioned witches, a coven. Maybe one of the local pagans would get the references.

She flipped back to the introductory page. One element of the organizational structure made sense. Six distinct sections divvied up the book's thousand-plus pages, and they aligned with some of the comments made by the ethereal visitor.

Dividing thin pages into chunks, Megan looked at the start of each section. Chapter headings designated air, spirit, and water, each element marked with a symbol. Following those three came a few thick, glossy pages filled with etchings of stick figures and handwritten notes.

The latter half of the book offered three more sections:

fire, earth, and chaos. Again, each one was paired with a marking made of loops, arrows, and curls.

She tapped a finger to her nose. Those three had to comprise the so-called dark trinity.

Directed by memories of the entity contact and curious to know more, she went to the fire section and studied the picture under the heading. A circle inside a square with a teardrop in the middle. Okay. On a hunch, she leafed to the beginning of the book and scanned the table of contents.

Her gaze landed on a drawing on the inside cover flap: a doodle identical to the fire circle. A possible lead. Might be prudent to focus her study on the fire section.

Her phone chimed, and she opened the text.

I'm here, I think. Please tell me you aren't sleeping in that obviously haunted asylum.

Megan smiled at Thom's dry wit. *It was an orphanage, and I'm in the bunkhouse. Be right over to let u in.*

She swung her legs and planted her feet on the floor, unable to stop a soft grunt as she willed her stiff body into an upright position. A gnarly fall and sitting hunched on a bed for hours had her feeling like she was turning to stone.

Anticipation lightening her steps, she tiptoed to the entrance and urged the door open with as much silent care as she could muster.

Dressed in a bomber jacket and jeans, Thom blazed a path through the assault of wintery precipitation. Though he moved with a predictable swagger that no doubt alerted all in a room to his importance, the hand he raised in greeting came up with a subtle hint of hesitation.

Megan rested the side of her head against the door jamb, intrigued by that small twitch in his wave. Was Thom James, the quintessential arrogant rock star, concerned that she might greet him with scorn or indifference?

He closed the remaining space between them with a few

big strides, a dark stocking cap giving way to the brown waves that grazed his strong jaw. As soon as he set foot on the doorstep, a car flashed high beams.

Thom looked back at his ride. "That's my driver. We found him a motel a mile down the road. I'll ring him as soon as you're ready for me to leave."

The first notes of his deep English accent, husky from smoking and trained to woo in a seductive, panty-dropping drawl, had her doubling down on resolve not to develop a crush on this man. Megan did *not* confuse sex with emotional attachment, and he wasn't even here for sex.

Yet she chanced a happy glance at the messenger bag he wore. He'd brought an overnight kit to the bunkhouse in lieu of sending his stuff to the motel with the driver.

"He can stay here, but there isn't an extra bed or blankets. So sorry." Which begged the question, where to put Thom? She didn't want to come off as presumptuous or pushy in case he didn't do repeat performances. Not that she was hoping to have sex.

"It's fine. He was looking forward to the Wi-Fi." Thom gave a thumbs-up in the direction of the car, and the driver took off in a cloud of sparkling snow.

They stood there for enough extra moments that time's passage became noticeable and awkward. He looked at her, then away, before reclaiming eye contact. A lopsided smile, one she would have categorized as shy if she didn't know who he was, tilted Thom's lips. "Good to see you again, Megan."

"Yeah. You too." Though she'd had her fair share of greetings like this, cursory words exchanged before the commencement of sweaty business, this time the exchange felt different. Unsure, a feeling out. Because they weren't here to fuck, to use the other person as means to a selfish end. She stepped aside. "Come in."

"Thank you, Megan."

She laughed. "You like saying my name, huh?"

His smile grew roguish, settling into a smug grin of victory. "Now that I finally know it, yes, I shall take great pleasure in repeating it."

She crossed her arms over her chest and narrowed her eyes in fake, jesting disdain. "Always in control, huh?"

With a wink, Thom brushed a chaste kiss to her cheek. The contrast of his warm breath and cool skin, tantalizing hints of aftershave and cigarette smoke, stimulated more than her senses as he moved past. A tingle chased over her as she imagined doing dirty things in the tiny bunk bed.

"Oh," he lowered his voice to a whisper while looking around. "There are others here."

She looked up into brown eyes that sparkled with mischief even in the nominal light from her reading lamp. "So? Were you hoping to get laid?"

"Absolutely. Always." He didn't miss a beat, and she laughed at the honesty, her shoulders loosening.

"We don't have to whisper." She moved her pitch up to a low purr. "These guys sleep like the dead." Megan walked to the bed and sat, scooting her body to the short edge aligned with the corner.

"Except you. It's well past midnight." He tapped the book with a single finger while joining her on the mattress and dropping his bag to the floor. "What's this?"

"Beats me." She pinched the corners of her eyes. "I found it while investigating the orphanage basement. I'll spare you the details."

He fluttered the long edges of the pages, reached into an internal pocket of the leather satchel, and produced the watch. Without a word, he handed it over.

"I appreciate you coming all this way for me." Their fingers brushed as she accepted her sacred keepsake, his callused hand warmer than she would have guessed.

The timepiece ticked in a steady pace, the weight in her palm as comforting as a hug from an old friend. On the face, six interlocking circles full of teeny, turning gears made for an intricate show of clockwork precision rendered in miniature. "This watch is the most important thing I own. Irreplaceable."

Nobody but her and the spirit of Gran knew that the devil was, literally, in the details. He lived in between all those little metal teeth that worked nonstop to keep evil energies trapped and moving in endless circles of frustration.

"I could tell by looking at it." He trained a long look on her face. "It's a gorgeous piece."

She wasn't sure if he dropped the double entendre with intent or if he'd practiced a seductive voice for so long it came as second nature.

His next words, though, were nearly brusque in their earnestness. "Are you ready to clarify the comment that you made in the hotel?"

"Yeah." Megan dragged her attention away from his scent and presence, from the ambient warmth of his body, and to the way her watch had gone bananas at the after-party. "Can you scoot closer so I can show you how this works?" She clipped her light to the headboard.

In a single, fluid motion, he was beside her, their hips and shoulders touching. When he leaned down to pull off his motorcycle boots, she watched how his body moved with a certain grace. She didn't peg Thom as someone trained in dance, but he did strike her as a person with layers. Not that his depths mattered one iota to the task at hand.

He was up against her again, so close that a piece of his hair grazed her ear. She pretended to ignore the ache between her legs, how fluttery and silly his proximity made her.

"See all of the circles full of gears?" Determined to win the battle against desire, she held the watch face directly under the light.

A quest for willpower became fumbling. What was the deal with this guy? Megan *never* got attached after sex and *so* rarely felt that inexplicable pull toward another human being, that sense of someone as more significant, more potent than scores of others. And Thom James, of all people? Please. This had to be some kind of stress reaction.

"Mm-hm." His damn throaty rumble reminded her that they sat at kissing distance.

She chanced a discreet sidelong glance in his direction, nearly succumbing upon catching how he seemed to study the side of her neck, his eyes hooded and lips parted. Megan swallowed, sure as hell knowing male desire when she spotted it.

But, as she also knew, this man was just plain horny all the time. His reputation along with the groupie gossip circuit testified to his nature.

With a roll of her shoulders, she steeled her resolve and directed Thom's distracting gaze to the watch by gliding her finger over the smooth glass. "My grandmother had a gift. We would speak to each other with our minds, and after we'd been doing that for a few years, she gave me this. She wouldn't tell me details of how she ended up with it, just generalities about destiny and being handed a task."

"What sort of task?" His rich voice was steeped in curiosity, and he grazed a thick finger over the leather band. She remembered those thick fingers. And the rest of him, long and almost obscenely thick.

A goofy chuckle, dorky in its attempt to mask her arousal, sprang from her lips. What a preposterous situation, trapped in an abandoned orphanage about to explain demon hunting to her rock star one-night stand. Yet here she was, in no hurry to jet. "I can do more than speak telepathically with my grandma."

"I'm listening."

A shudder raced over her skin as memories darkened.

As if possessing the empathy necessary to read her flash of distress, he touched her forearm in a gesture more tender than flirtatious. "My apologies. Would you rather not go into this?"

"No. It's fine. You need the context for what I'm about to say to make sense. Starting when I was six, I would see a shadow standing at the edge of my bed. Eight feet tall, upright, but no distinct legs or other features." She swallowed thickly, committed to keeping her outward mask of bravery secured even as she hugged that scared little girl within. "It would just stand there, this smoky stuff rising off of it, while I lay in bed paralyzed."

"Oh, Megan," Thom whispered. "That's awful."

"I'd wake up to it. Not every night either, the pattern was totally random. And every time I assumed it had left, it would come back. Like this monster was torturing me psychologically. Always my bed too. Never my brother's." Hurt and anger ripped off an old scar. The terrified, embittered girl clawed to Megan's surface. "Never in the five years we shared a room."

"This went on for five years?" He held her hand.

She covered her face with her opposite palm, the watch dangling from her fingers like some hexed talisman, the external marker of her curse. The meaty organ inside her chest wrenched, hot and tender from wounds unhealed. "Yeah. I'd get so pissed off after awhile, so resentful. I hated that I was a girl and made up this fantasy that if I was a boy like my brother, the menace would leave. I even made my parents sign me up for this coed football league, even though

I sucked at it. I thought that if I started acting like a boy, the monster would leave me alone."

Memories spun together until a toxic soup filled her head. Adventures in having sex like a man hadn't always worked out so great either, often hurling invisible footballs that struck her pride and emotions instead of bloodying her nose.

Silence stretched long and wide while Thom offered strokes of comfort. His steady breathing centered her, and she spoke when the pause became too much to endure.

"I'm regressing, I'm sorry." Words came out in a huff as she lowered her hand, admittedly feeling unburdened. "Thank you for humoring me. I'm a total disaster who needs fixing."

"Please don't apologize." He slipped a hand to her cheek and angled her face until their eyes met. A liquid sheen to his brown eyes betrayed emotional connection and compassion. They gave evidence of a search too, an investigation into what lay behind her wall. "You're perfect how you are."

Right about now was when she normally inched away emotionally. Men had tried to get close in the past, made moves to turn their involvement into more than sex. Those men earned themselves a sarcastic remark and directions to the nearest exit.

Not one thing about the present moment was normal, though, and her brief yet destabilizing entanglement with Thom was a different species of encounter than past hookups. Though his smoothness kindled a pang of worry, a fear that she was being played, Megan allowed that tiny spark to die. No longer the ballsy initiator, the proud, brash slut, Megan surrendered. She closed her eyes and nodded, tendering consent for whatever he asked for.

The first graze of his lips was barely perceptible, a whisper of moisture and pressure carried on calm breath.

A small noise left her lips as a hum of not altogether

sexual desire, strange and bathed in frightful openness, seeped from her chest to her extremities. The overwhelming nature of this rapture was too much, and not enough. She tried to speak. Words failed.

One came at last: "Yes."

What transpired was a kiss, but so much more than any kiss she'd shared until now. His lips caressed hers, top and bottom, massaging care into her mouth as if he possessed the power to bring her home. Even when tongue arrived in a gentle slide, the addition was seeking, not lusty.

Not insistent, never shoving or probing. Not a step on the road to fucking like most of her kisses since the first one.

No, Thom kissed for the moment, explored her interior like he had nowhere to be. The kiss was a kiss was a kiss, such a simple and profound concept as to be divine.

When she responded to him, her own ministrations given in an unhurried manner, a chunk of stone inside of her crumbled.

This was it, what it meant to *be* with someone, checked in and present. Twin tears slipped from her eyes, and he caught one with the pad of his thumb like the droplet was some tiny creature in need of saving.

When her gentler feelings at last overwhelmed her, Megan moaned into Thom's mouth and pressed herself to him. Masculine lust sounded off in the noise he uttered right back. The stiff ridge against her hip left no doubt.

Who was she kidding? He wanted to fuck. A hard cock lacked a conscience, as she'd known since age thirteen.

Her wall entered full rebuild mode, and she fisted the sides of his shirt before moving busy fingers to undo his button and zipper. Time to steer this into a more predictable and well-trod region.

Maintaining the lip lock, she smirked against his mouth while reaching into his pants and circling a firm, no-fail grip around his silken bar of flesh. Unsurprising, how he went commando. She stroked him, the pads of her fingers and thumb lavishing rubs on his ridge and crown on the upstroke.

"You like that, huh?" The rhetorical question was for the sake of further exciting him, as the answer was obvious.

Thom broke the kiss and gently extracted her from his jeans. "Of course, but I thought we could just kiss tonight. A proper first kiss."

Megan pursed her make-out swollen lips, marinating in an exhausting combination of gratitude and resentment all wrapped in humiliation-glazed vulnerability. She had a ton of emotions she didn't want to unpeel along with the symbolism of their quite *improper* actual first kiss. "I don't really do soft and sweet."

"Neither do I." He stroked her jawline with a callused thumb. "But I rather love it with you."

"I think we should stick to talking about the watch." Absurd to say, as they couldn't un-eat the sandwich they'd shared seconds ago.

"Uh, Megan?" Gary's bemused drawl landed like pin to bubble. "Why is there a famous musician in your bunk?"

FOUR

THOM HAD WALTZED INTO THE ROLE OF OTHER MAN PLENTY
of times, thanks to the horny frenzy of an adult life spent on
the shag and unconcerned with consequences. He'd lost
count of the number of times he'd breezed out of some
woman's bedroom, zipping up his pants and barely finished
coming, when a boyfriend or husband darkened the door in
advance of his scheduled return.

And in those moments, he'd merely shrugged and kept on
walking while some cuckold stood there agog. He'd never
cared about a woman enough to fight for her. The emotion of
jealousy was alien to him.

Until now.

Thom sized up this Gary bloke. Spindly muscles,
submissive energy, tell-tale gape of the starstruck. The way he
dumped his weight onto one foot and plucked at his t-shirt
did not communicate alpha stature. Threat level: zero.

In a way, Gary's humility before a superior specimen
twisted the knife deeper into Thom's guts. What did Megan
see in this git?

"So sorry," Thom said in a smooth tone that wasn't

particularly apologetic, his half-smile smug by intent. "Did we wake you?"

"No, I just got up for a leak, and wow. Here you are, Thom James, in the bed below me. I'm floored. I'm a huge fan of you guys. *Icarus's Wing* was brilliant. Your ability to adapt and reinvent never ceases to amaze me."

Envy morphed to amusement, then to mild contempt. The lad sure had rolled over and shown his underbelly without so much as a halfhearted attempt to posture. He must've known he was beat, but by not fighting for a prize like Megan, he automatically squandered Thom's respect.

"Thank you." He put his arm around Megan's soft, warm body, not caring about the undone state of his fly. They had nothing to hide. "Would you excuse us, please?"

"You bet." Gary scratched the top of his head. "Would you mind signing my planner?"

Thom schooled his face into neutrality and swallowed a derisive snort. Yikes, the cuckold role suited this one. He circled a lazy hand on Megan's back and smelled her hair. "Sure, mate. In the morning, I'd be happy to."

"Thanks." After showing a toothy smile, Gary trucked off to the restroom.

Megan shook her head and laid the back of her hand over her mouth, muting a cute giggle.

"What?" He spoke into her silky hair, inhaling that night magic smell of hers that damn near drugged him into a stupor.

"You assumed we were together," she whispered, her eyes narrowing.

"Aren't you?"

"Nope." An odd pause after her statement gave *him* pause. "But?"

"Now and then I think he might still have a thing for me." She nestled into his hold, her move to get closer obliterating any lingering temptation to fret that Gary mattered anymore. "Besides, I was never dating him. Just doing him."

"Ah, I see. Was he as good as me?"

She rolled her eyes. "Ego check."

A toilet flushed. When Thom heard footsteps, he hushed his voice to a whisper in an attempt to spare a nominal scrap of the approaching man's pride. "We both know he wasn't."

She slugged him in the ribs.

He feigned injury to amuse her, clutching his side theatrically.

Her smile inspired him to kiss her nose like he did at the hotel. Megan made him feel so genuine, like a complete person. He adored her for that, for how she brought out a secret joy in him. A part of him that was so real but difficult to square with his cocky persona. Nice to have a break from that character, from the mask he'd worn so long it had fused painfully to his head in a skewed tilt.

Gary climbed the bunk ladder, tossed and turned for a bit, and fell silent after a groan.

"Step out for a smoke?" Thom asked.

"I'm supposed to be quitting," she said in a throaty, bad girl voice that he enjoyed. The other, sexy devil side of Megan.

"Me too." He only lit up after sex, decent progress when he once cultivated a pack a day habit, though the sex rule still meant that he was sparking between one and three per day. "How about we quit together starting tomorrow. We can be accountability buddies."

Her look was sly. "If I was prone to flattering myself, I'd say you were making up reasons for us to keep in touch."

He tucked a strand of hair behind her ear, lost to the exquisite curve of her face. Doll features with a bold chin to give her countenance character. Perfect. "You should flatter yourself more. Otherwise, I'll be forced to do it for you, and I can get rather sappy."

"No sap allowed. Let's step out."

He rolled out of the bunk and fished a soft pack of smokes and lighter from the overnight bag he mentally congratulated himself for packing. After tugging on his boots, he held her hand as they ventured out into the frosty night.

He pushed open the door to an ice palace of beauty. The blizzard had ebbed at last, leaving their dot of rural darkness draped in porcelain. He sparked and drew down sweet tobacco smoke along with chilled, humid air, content for the first time in ages. If only he and Megan had hot chocolate and a fireplace, he'd be in heaven.

"Why is it so quiet after a big snow?" A teasing wind animating the ends of her hair, winter flames that danced through the dark as she spoke.

He passed her the cigarette. "No clue. I've lived in Los Angeles for twenty-five years. Well, mostly. I own properties in Hawaii and Maine. Go on holiday there a few times a year." One fast glance in her direction turned up no evidence that she was impressed by his assets. His heart dropped a notch. "I'm thinking of renting a flat in Paris as well."

"Silence has a texture." She blew out her drag with a hiss through pursed lips, a faraway and pensive cast overtaking her profile. The woman was fit to be painted, her image hung in the finest museum. "Especially when combined with solitude. It…flexes. If you listen closely, you can hear those beyond the veil. They come out at night. When it's still."

She handed over the smoke, and he used his drag as an excuse to ride a cautious beat. Best to approach the subject she clearly needed to talk about with a blend of sensitivity and directness. "Like the shadow person came out to stand by your bedside?"

"Yeah." Her resigned tone made him hurt and yearn for

her. For recompense, or peace, or some other sort of closure on this frightening formative incident. "I think I feel shitty about it all sometimes because my inception into supernatural communication wasn't good. The first visitor I met wasn't a person, or what remained of a person or whatever, and it wanted to scare me. Make me feel despair."

"I'm so sorry. What eventually happened to it?"

"I told Gran, and that's when she explained my so-called gift of sight. The first night I put the watch by my bed, the gears went crazy, and this insane buzzing sound started throbbing in my neck. But that was the end of the shadow person."

"So now you track and trap these entities for the general benefit of others?"

She flicked her wrist in a scooping motion, and he provided the cigarette. The cherry crackled orange in a controlled inferno as Megan's cheeks hollowed like she couldn't imbibe nicotine fast enough. "Yeah. Though now money drives me more than ever." A pointed edge to her consonants and hard emphasis on the syllables in money hinted at a helpless, grief-stricken type of anger.

He cocked his head, and the aggression with which she smashed the depleted smoke underfoot did not slip past him. Best to offer an ear but not pry into her personal life. As much as a drive to know her business and help in any way tugged on him, pushy caveman antics served no one. "May I ask why money is newly important?"

She looked at her shoes, puffy snow boots whose astronaut aesthetic evidenced her practical smarts. No high-heeled mincing on ice for Megan.

"I got fired." Though she spoke the fact plainly, sadness slipped through in the overcompensation of her drawling monotone. "Well, technically I didn't get tenure. I have a few more months of salary and health insurance to look forward to. As long as I can face my colleagues for the duration of my employment there."

Elements of this did not sit right with him. He caught shame and rage in her tone, though not culpability. "I am so terribly sorry. Want to talk about it?"

She scoffed. "It's embarrassing. Humiliating, actually." A lingering glance invited him to nudge forward.

"No judgment here." He had a plethora of shameful, embarrassing stories stashed in his memory roster.

Megan jammed her hands into her pockets, her shoulders tensing. "I was messing around with the department chair. Fucking him, to be precise. Some of the other faculty found out and complained that I was getting special treatment. Which I wasn't, but whatever. Once they had me in their crosshairs, they figured out how to invalidate a few key items on my tenure file. A journal I published in was suddenly deemed too far afield to count. I suspect that someone hacked my teaching evaluations and flooded them with low scores to tank my average. But I can't prove it."

Clobbered by the injustice here, Thom wrapped his head around a glaring omission. "What about him?"

She quirked a brow. "Who?"

He threw his hands in the air, outraged. "This department chair. Was he fired as well?"

She unleashed a bitter chuckle devoid of humor. "Nope. It doesn't work that way."

"Why the hell not?" Even in the frigid air, his scalp sizzled.

"Um, hello, double standards. He's a stud, I'm a slut. I saw the looks these same people gave him, and they weren't the leering smirks reserved for me."

Fury pulled him into molten riptide. "This is absolutely outrageous."

"It's fine. It's over at least."

"No." Hooting winds sang a chorus of agreement as he laid a hand on Megan's elbow. "It is not."

"How do you figure?" She glanced at him askance, though a lilt in her voice gave away curiosity. "What do you plan to do, march in there and demand he reinstate me while shouting 'do you know who I am'?"

"I don't have a plan yet," Thom admitted. "But that might change after a good night's sleep."

"Well, thank you for thinking of me." She said it like the thoughtfulness of others was a gift she'd rarely enjoyed.

"You're worth it. Worthy."

Megan hummed and surrendered eye contact, fidgeting with her sleeve. For all her brazen behavior, it occurred to Thom that deep down she might want for true strength. Confidence to replace bravado.

He took her face in both hands and captured her gaze. "I mean that. And I'm sorry for how I took advantage of you. Used you. I messed up, and I'll try to do better next time."

"You didn't take advantage or use me. I'm an adult, I knew what I was doing, and I made my choices."

Despite her assurance, he didn't want to let himself off the hook too easy. He'd leveraged his fame and power to get sex from a vulnerable woman who deserved more than some sleazy hookup with a dirty rocker. Megan deserved love—love he didn't have to give. He had respect to give her though. Empathy and support. Kindness. Friendship.

"I still think there's no excuse for how I treated you." Like a generic, nameless groupie to be fucked and forgotten. Unacceptable.

She grabbed his hands and moved them to her waist. "I like how you treated me."

Memories of their tryst in the hotel flooded him with arousal despite the recent attunement of his shiny, new moral compass. "Slow. Let's take this slow."

"Why? I want you, you want me. What's wrong with giving in?"

He sighed. "I've never taken things slow with anyone is all. Never bothered to get to know a woman I was attracted to before."

Never had to. When sex came free and easy, nonstop pussy splaying open multiple times per day since that first tour over thirty years ago, Thom quickly opted for quantity over quality. Groupies were an inexhaustible resource, ever-present and always ready to go.

He'd gotten lazy almost immediately, fallen into a rut, and only begun to question his own behavior when he stopped being able to deny that he felt like garbage when the deed was done. He spent too much time feeling guilty and polluted by the distinct revulsion of using a stranger's body to get off.

Time for a change, beginning now.

With the chunky toe of her boot, she made a circle in the dusting of snow. "Our alignment is skewed. I sort of hate that."

"What alignment?"

"Oh, you know. I'm hardly the good girl counterpoint to your rakish ways, conveniently equipped to show you by way of my chastity and intelligence how a wholesome woman is the answer to your problems."

Endeared to her more and more with each passing second, her irreverent charm guarding a soft quality, Thom edged to the precipice of a limit. "I'm not sure if there is an answer to my problems, but wholesomeness and chastity don't interest me in the slightest. Those aren't virtues. They're prisons."

"I don't know if I agree. There's value in restraint. Moderating the appetites and all. Keeping them in check."

He hadn't thought about it that way. He might be squandering his energy in all those late nights full of empty sex. "I suppose that's one explanation of why I feel so tired much of the time. Burned out and spent."

"I feel that way a lot too. Scattered. Fried. I've wondered before if all the sex I've had has blown out too many of my good brain chemicals. Turned me into a dopamine junkie."

An especially fierce gust sliced through the thin material of his jeans. "Hold that thought. Ready to head in?"

"What, you don't want to make snow angels? 'Cause of the irony of, you know, us being angels?"

He kissed the frosty point of her nose. "Good one. But if it's all the same, can we connect with our inner five-year-olds some other time? Because I think ice crystals might actually be forming in my bone marrow."

"You need to visit me in these Midwestern parts more often, Mr. Los Angeles. Toughen up." Her flaming waves chased the wind as she opened the bunkhouse door, her smirk casting pretend aspersions.

"Fair enough. I have a possible compromise." Upon reentering the room, he rubbed his chilled hands together.

"Do tell." She knocked her boots against the wall, toed them off, and got comfortable in the bunk.

"Is there a skating rink nearby? We'll hit the ice, then have hot chocolate."

Megan crawled under the covers and patted the spot beside her. "That's the most wholesome date anyone has asked me on, ever."

Thom assumed his cherished spot next to her. "That's the most wholesome date I've asked anyone on."

"I thought wholesomeness was a prison."

"I'll make an exception for ice skating."

Besides, when was the last time he'd asked a woman out for dinner, a movie, or ice skating? Had to be in secondary school, back in London, back when he actually had to try. He hadn't been on a proper date since that first tour, when he'd unleashed his insatiable id and never bothered to rein it in.

He'd missed so much, wasted so much in those years—who was he kidding, *decades*—spent sticking his dick into women and not giving one fart where they went or what happened to them after he blew his load.

Sure, he'd had fun, lived it up like only a rock star could, though now he wondered if he'd shot out too much of his heart or soul along with all that cum.

The women deserved better, that part of the minor epiphany was easier to accept.

Harder to grasp was the sober realization that he, too, deserved better. Deserved more. Deserved the person beside him.

"You got pensive." Megan rested her chin on his chest, searching his face for some insight.

He stroked the delicate curvature of her spine, getting to know her body caress by stroke.

All those spots he'd overlooked, he touched. The freckles on her cheeks, the way her earlobes fused. How soft the skin under her arm felt like silk-dipped velvet.

When she pulled her sweater over her head and threw it to the floor, leaving her in a tank top, he asked, "What's the meaning behind your tattoo?" There had to be a story in that vibrant jungle of plants and flowers.

"It's dumb." Her cheeks pinked, and she pulled a thin blanket to her neck.

"I doubt it. But I won't press if you'd rather not say."

"The piece is meant to represent the Garden of Eden before the fall. So even though I'm a fallen woman, I have a reminder that there was once a sacred and pure space." One shoulder kicked up in a hesitant shrug. "Maybe even still. Inside of me."

This struck him as incredibly sad, this burden she carried

that she'd surrendered or forsaken a treasure she once possessed. Doubly unfair, given how little sleep he'd lost or angst he suffered over his own promiscuity. Had men like this foul department chair, and her colleagues, had a hand in picking at her insecurities?

Likely, but right now they didn't matter. She did. He tipped her chin up with two fingers. "Of course, it's there. That pure space never left."

She closed her eyes, pale lashes making fans near her cheeks, and said in a shaky whisper, "I don't just mean sleeping around. I think that shadow person took something from me. Something that I can't define or explain. But since that happened, I haven't been the same."

He considered her point. "Is that why you got into paranormal investigations? Trapping demons? To try and seal off these energies before they took any more from you?"

"That sounds right. And now, apparently, I have more work to do. But I'm desperate for a break from it all. Tell me about you. Your life story."

So he did, eager to oblige. He told her of his early years in London, befriending the other members of Fyre when they were all scrappy outsiders thrust for one reason or another into an elite secondary school where they didn't belong. Thom told the story of Fyre's discovery at the school talent show and the whirlwind of madness that followed as the fame machine blasted them to the top of the summit.

He told her of the disappointment his academic parents felt when he didn't go into politics or law, their emotional withdrawal and how deeply that hurt him as an only child with no siblings to turn to for comfort. How, perhaps, that first betrayal sent him into the bed of woman after woman, seeking to replicate that first high of sexual release in a misguided effort to fill the hole in his heart. He told her how his music and songwriting filled some of the hole, but that space remained.

Once he realized she'd nodded off, he fluffed his pillow, closed his eyes, and drifted.

Unbidden, Thom's eyes snapped open. The bed was shaking, vibrating, with a powerful hum that damn near rattled his teeth. His heart thundered as blood roared in his ears, adrenaline burning anxiously from fingertips to toes. What the fuck was happening?

Once his vision adjusted, he saw. A black blob, easily seven-feet tall and shaped in some messy prototype of a human form, loomed at the foot of the bed. He strained to leap up to defend Megan and himself but didn't budge an inch, leaving him useless against a bleak onslaught of fear and despair.

FIVE

A scream died in Megan's throat. She was awake but immobile. Paralyzed. A familiar menace, dark and blobby, stared her down from the foot of the bed.

He's back.

She thrashed and yelled, willing herself to wake up even though her body was as heavy as lead and her throat was too thick to let the sounds go. The shadow crawled up her frozen legs as adrenaline coursed through her veins, begging her to run. Finally, she shoved a sound out of her throat. It came out as a pitiful moan, but any noise was a start. She could wake herself up if she kept shouting, so she did.

After what felt like an eternity, she wrenched her eyes open. Sweat pasted her hair to the back of her neck, and her heart hammered. The shadow figure was gone.

She slid to the end of the bunk bed, shimmying between Thom's sleeping form and the wall, and planted bare soles on the frigid tile floor in some effort to ground herself. Her nasty old friend had returned, but at least he didn't have a strong toehold in the waking world. She buried her face in her hands until the sour queasiness roiling her stomach subsided. She was safe and okay. For now.

Why, after all these years, had the demon come back? What triggered the entity's return?

She slouched and cradled her head in her hands, peering at the table of equipment out of the corner of her eye. Occam's Razor would suggest that the prior night's investigation somehow loosened the malevolent energy. Her only problem was the lack of a theory to put in that "somehow" blank.

"You okay?" Stationed at the table, Lindsay looped cords in a figure eight and tucked devices into black bags.

Dressed in jeans with her wet hair a bun, the other woman was perky and ready to face the day, an awkward contrast highlighting Megan's zombie status.

"Fine. Just didn't sleep well." Megan padded to the gear station and assisted her colleague in packing out. Smells of plastic and the crunch of Velcro comforted her while the pair worked, a mundane routine helping her forget the sleep disturbance.

"You woke up in the middle of the night, moaning and screaming." Pieces came apart with tidy snicks as Lindsay, trying to sound casual, removed a battery.

"I get night terrors," Megan muttered, fumbling with a microphone.

"Even with the sexy bassist in your bed?" The teasing sing-song inflection made Megan smile, but barely.

"Apparently." She looked around the room until a change of subject opportunity arose. "Where are the guys?"

"They drove into town. There's a coffee shop with Wi-Fi. Greg was hot to email your footage to the sponsor. If it's okay with you, I'm actually gonna pack the rest of this in my car and go join them. I'm dying without my morning caffeine injection. Wanna come, or are you inclined to have private time with the rocker?"

Megan knew Lindsay well enough to bet that she was excusing herself so as not to be a third wheel with Thom around but didn't want to make Megan feel uncomfortable or obligated to refute by saying so. Lindsay's maturity and tactful approach to loyalty ranked high among her admirable traits.

"I'm good here. Go for it." Megan lined up cases in a tidy row on the tabletop.

"Are you sure you're alright?" Lindsay scrunched her eyebrows, concern in her dark eyes. "You seem a little weary and distracted."

No point in lying to Lindsay, who saw through fibs like they were cellophane cling wrap. "I can't get my head around that book. And the nightmare I had was an old recurring one from my childhood." The air seemed to leave the room, the basic surroundings popping into sharp relief as Megan prepared her creepy follow-up. "Have you ever found an object during one of these investigations and later regretted taking it?"

"As in angered some otherworldly force by removing this hypothetical object?"

"Exactly."

Lindsay's eyes slid up to the left as if she was scanning her bank for memories. "No. But then again, ghosts don't tend to form attachments to corporeal objects unless they died grieving another person. Ghosts are strictly place-bound critters. You know this." The blonde played with her hair, a grimace darkening her features. "Unless you aren't talking about the spirit remnant of a dead human."

"Right." Her mouth dried as she faced Lindsay's mixture of worry and befuddlement.

"What's going on?" Lindsay took a step back.

Megan dug her fingertips into her temples. "The watch

that Thom returned to me...it's hard to explain. It traps demons. I pick up their wavelength now and then on these expeditions. They try to gain control of me, and I send them into the watch. They get stuck in the gears."

Lindsay stared at her.

Frustration tightened Megan's muscles as she folded her arms over her chest, floundering in the crosshairs of Lindsay's disturbed expression. "Well, what did you think was going on down there?" She pointed in the direction of the orphanage basement. "With me levitating upside down and hitting the floor, all of Gary's talk of possession?"

"I don't know." Lindsay shook her head. "At first, I thought it was theatrics you pulled off somehow, then I chalked it up to a freak occurrence. Like the time Chris started speaking in tongues."

Ghosts desperate for a connection to the earthly plane could get as far as scrambling a person's brain waves to make contact, as in the case of Chris's brief conscription as a channel. But Megan's experience had gone beyond that. "This thing took over my body, Linds. Guided me to the book."

Lindsay paled. "Then you shouldn't have taken that book."

"You aren't being especially helpful right now, Captain Obvious."

"Okay. Fair. I apologize." On a deep breath, Lindsay steepled her fingers underneath her lips. "If the watch traps the demons, what's the problem?"

"The nightmare I had involves an old-school demon. It *was* trapped, but now I'm worried that it's back out."

"Has it ever done anything to you besides give you night terrors?"

"No." But this book hadn't been a factor in the equation back then either.

"Then you probably don't have a thing to worry about."

Lindsay checked her nonmagical, electronic watch. Awareness of the humdrum gizmo provoked an irrational bout of jealousy. "Hey, I gotta run. Call me if you need to talk, alright?" She filled her arms with bags and got a move on.

"Bye," Megan said as the door closed behind Lindsay. She mitigated the sting of rejection by rationalizing that she might have done the same thing had the roles been reversed.

While Thom slept, his forearm over his eyes, Megan slipped the book out from under the bed, quizzical upon noticing how the cover popped up and the pages didn't lay flat.

When she glimpsed a gap between pages near the end, she cleaved the tome to the bookmarked place. Her organs leapt and tumbled on a wave of shock and mild horror. Her watch marked a spot near the back of the volume. As her horizon contracted to the odd, unsettling discovery, Megan picked up her watch and zeroed in on networks of gears.

They hummed along in their diligent, endless circumferences—except one. The gears of the first circle in the arch of six didn't budge. Their coloring looked wrong too, not the normal shades of bronze and silver. Her body temperature cooling, Megan pulled the timepiece an inch from her face and confirmed a sinking suspicion. They were discolored alright. Brown and corroded with rust.

"Chaos rides fire to Folly's reign." The voice in Megan's head spoke so quietly, the faintest ephemeral whisper, as to obfuscate tone, gender, and any other identifiable qualities.

"What does that mean?" Though Megan imagined her speech as even and unbothered, she felt her teeth clench and heard tension in her cadence. She'd done a stupid, terrible thing down in that basement.

Ethereal, trilling laughter sounded off in some distant recess of Megan's mind.

"Are you connected to the shadow at the foot of my bed?"

Sweat slicked her palms and underarms as she braced herself for an affirmative reply.

"I ate it." Contempt oozed thick.

"To protect me?" The feeble, absurd question landed in a pathetic upswing as the final scraps of hope for some positive outcome slipped through Megan's fingers.

"To use you. To feed *me*." The speech faded to near-nonexistence, forcing Megan to strain in efforts to make out more. "I am weak but will be strong. Folly summons chaos. Fire is fuel."

"As was the shadow person. Fuel."

"Demons and fire are food."

"Who are you?"

"Folly. Too weak now. Soon will be strong. Mighty." With that final, chilling declaration, the guest's distinct words blended into the background hum of Megan's hearing.

Alone again with her own unnerved, pessimistic thoughts, Megan had a gander at the part of the page where the watch had lain. The spot directly underneath it was some kind of sigil comprised of loopy swirls and forbidding, jagged points like barbed wire. The symbol didn't make any sense to her, but a paragraph of text preceding the etching did. Perhaps the information there would help her decipher the drawing. Wincing in preemptive displeasure, she read:

A practitioner of chaos magic wishing to summon and control demons for her own benefit must stay aware of the costs, for dealing in this infernal realm will forever spoil her goodness and sanctity of mind. If you agree to the terms, practitioner, beware. Once these hideous creatures are afoot on her accord, the chaos witch becomes bound to their foul whims and malevolent agendas. They will stick to her the same as viscous tentacles suctioned to the folds of her brain, tormenting and confusing for their own capricious entertainment. Expect madness and utter degradation of self and dignity. Upon acceptance of this cursed union, a chaos witch may take and wield the evil with moderate control.

Fuck. She wiped her palms on her sweatpants. Had she consented to this awfulness in some way? She certainly didn't have any recollection of doing so. The only part of the reading saving her from descending into total despair were the parts about acceptance, agreement, and wishing. She hadn't done any of those things.

Plus, there was, ya know, the whole thing about being a witch. Megan was, decidedly, not a witch. A nervous giggle eked from her, and she drew in a long breath and blew it out in a cooling exhale. "You're fine." She didn't feel fine, but whatever. Just anxiety and nerves talking.

Despite her efforts to chill, the next peek she hazarded at the symbol was unfocused and cautious, like the print might leap from the book and poke out her eyes. Reading the blurb hadn't explained the drawing any better, yet she lost herself in those curves and swirls capped in knife points. Her perception dreamy and faraway, she followed lines until they dead-ended, soon grasping that the etched labyrinth her watch had just ended up on was just that—a maze. Leading where?

Fighting the seduction of the pleasurable trance, she dropped her awareness to an italicized line of writing printed right beneath the picture.

Figure 13: Doorway to the exiled. Chaos witch shall place her cursed talisman upon the above rune and enter advanced state of meditation. Once she walks with the damned, she may choose a dark soul(s) for her consort and bind them to her will.

Her heart slammed. She hadn't done any of that, but the watch—a good candidate for a cursed talisman—ended up presumably serving as a key to this doorway all the same.

Megan looked bleakly into space. "What have you done?"

The bunk bed's old springs creaked as Thom cleared his

throat. "Megan, love, are you alright? I may have to ask you not to tell me any more scary stories before bed. Whew. The power of suggestion is strong."

She closed the book as gingerly as her nerves would allow, pushed it back under the bunk, and wrapped her watch in a t-shirt. If Thom had seen the shadow being too, like he was implying, that could mean it was getting stronger. But she didn't have any evidence of that and didn't want to scare him, so best to keep her worries to herself. She tucked the swaddled time piece into her duffel and silently begged the object not to get up to any more weirdness without her permission. "Fine, just straightening some things out." Banishing all creepiness from her mind, Megan jammed herself into normal-person mode and joined Thom on the bed. "Everyone else left. Want to get out of here?"

"Sure." He kissed her forehead, and she centered herself with the comforting fragrance of his smell. "When was the last time you ate a proper meal?"

Her stomach twisted around whatever remained of the chips. "Honestly? Sometime during Obama's second term."

"Those were the days." He rolled off the mattress, snatching up his overnight sack en route to the bathroom. Water ran from the sink. "There's a grocery store where you live, right? If it's alright with you, I'd like to cook you a meal. See your flat. Apartment, as you say here."

With any luck, a day spent in the company of a man she liked would neutralize the debacle that began in the basement, or at least provide enough distraction for her to gain perspective and decide what to do. "Excellent plan."

Possessions collected, including a certain hell-book weighing down her bag like a millstone around her neck, she left the bunkhouse with her hand snuggled protectively in Thom's large, warm grip. Clear blue skies domed the snow globe on the ground, a fresh, crisp day bringing good tidings.

What a cheerful, sunny winter day. Had to be a good sign. *Please, God, bring a fucking good omen.*

"Can I ask you an off the wall question?" Thom's breath puffed out as vapor, his tone a little too breezy.

"You bet." Snow crunched beneath her rubber soles as they trekked to her car, the sole vehicle in the parking lot. A power line was piled with white stuff, sprinklings falling to the ground as a squirrel walked the tightrope in cute, whimsical steps. Good omens, good tidings, good day.

"Do you sleepwalk?"

Megan was a hair's breadth away from cursing the Lord's name. But that probably wouldn't help this demon situation one iota.

"No. Why?" When they reached her Toyota, she fumbled in a pocket for her keys and jammed the right one in the lock with a bit more force than warranted. At least it didn't break off, trapping them at the orphanage.

"I had a strange dream involving the shadow person you described standing at the foot of the bed." An over-affected shrug from Thom as he went to the passenger's side. "I suppose that your story primed my subconscious."

She got in, unlocked his door, and started the engine. "Which has what to do with me sleepwalking?" Her sour tone made her flinch. "Sorry. I didn't mean to snark at you. I'm a little burned out on all things spooky."

"I apologize. I should have known. Never mind." While she pulled out and set off down the highway, he tapped on a cell phone screen. "I'm making a shopping list. What's the best grocery near here?"

Thoughts of an easygoing afternoon over a scrumptious brunch retreated from the forefront of her mind. She clenched the steering wheel. "On second thought, I want to hear it. Why you asked about sleepwalking."

"I had a bizarre dream was all. I didn't mean to alarm you

by insinuating there was a greater importance. Let's just chalk it up to my outsized ego assuming that my dreams matter in some cosmic sense."

His attempt at dismissal by self-deprecation didn't land. She heard it in his clipped and overly formal tone, how he kicked himself for letting the cat out of the bag while praying that she wasn't stubborn enough to press the issue.

"No, I don't think it's a good idea to blithely write off anything that implicates this shadow being. Please. Say."

A brief pause seemed to last for eons, Megan counting seconds like sheep as they rode in silence, the car a cloister of morbid anticipation as it passed by the normal happenings of country life. A man pushed a snow blower, a white arc spewing from the machine. A truck passed her, the driver oblivious to her existential dread.

"I closed my eyes, and when I opened them, the entity was gone." Thom spoke right as she was seriously considering screaming to relieve some tension. "But then you had taken its place at the foot of the bed. You just stood there, staring at me, with this blank look on your face. You were gone."

SIX

ONCE MORE, THOM FOUND HIMSELF SEATED HELPLESSLY IN Megan's presence, cursing his mistakes.

This had to be karma mocking him again. In the span of less than twenty-four hours, he'd changed from a man who cared only about women's lives and feelings insofar as caring got him laid to one who worried about them to the detriment of his own well-being.

This time, as they drove down a humble commercial street in silence and pulled into a grocery store parking lot, he isolated the blunt nature of his comment as the chief variable responsible for driving her away.

While she maneuvered her car between two trucks, he pried his foot from his mouth. "I shouldn't have said anything about the sleepwalking. I didn't mean to upset you."

People had called him too direct in the past, accused him of being abrasive and blunt. He ought to have listened, though he'd never bothered to modify his behavior for the sake of another person.

He was Thom James. They could deal with him or disappear. Mostly they dealt.

She turned off the ignition and afforded him a long, tired look. "I'm not upset. Just exhausted. I can't get my head around any of this, but I keep trying to until my brain feels like mush. And every new fact or detail freaks me out more without offering a glimpse at that elusive eureka moment." For emphasis, Megan snapped her fingers and crossed her eyes.

He smiled at her articulate statement delivered in deadpan, how she made fun of herself in such a disarming manner. Megan was so special. Too bad he lacked the means to help. "Do you know anyone who might be able to make sense of the book, if you brought it to them?"

Her lips twitched as if she chewed on her cheek. "There's a lady in town who owns a pagan store. Sells crystals and whatnot. It's a long shot, but I could take it to her and see what she says. Explain the incident with the watch and all the other stuff."

"Meaning how you forgot the watch at my hotel? Or how it supposedly detected bad energy around my band?" Mentioning Fyre ushered in a skitter of mild anxiety. The lads had to be wondering about him by now. When was their next show scheduled? Two days from now?

He'd call one of them after brunch so they didn't think he'd gone AWOL.

"Yeah." She spoke like she had more to say, meandering on the second syllable, before clamping her lips into a sharp smile. "Shall we head inside?"

Though the pauses between her words snagged him, as did her rapid changing of the subject, he wasn't about to interrogate her like some douche with a habit of trampling all over another person's boundaries. He knew when to pull back, how to stop himself from turning into an absolute arse. With as much tact as he could marshal, he forwarded, "As long as you know that you can talk to me."

"I appreciate that." Her face hidden behind a curtain of red hair, she collected her purse and swung her legs outside the car.

At this point, all he had to offer was support. Megan would give him no more or no less than she deemed fit, and he had to make peace with this fact. Taking careful steps over hard-packed snow, he laid a hand on her lower back to guard her against slip and fall hazards. "What do you feel like? Pancakes? Omelet? Or do you want to go the lunch route?"

"It's not that I don't want to talk with you about what happens to me..." She trailed off, her words dissolving into the January air on a pensive note.

"But?" They approached the market's entrance, and Thom accepted a grocery buggy from a uniform-clad teenage boy with an Afro.

The kid's jaw dropped as his eyes stretched. "Are you...? Holy shit, holy shit. You are Thom James. For real."

No escaping this one. His mind on Megan, Thom listened, with the best performance of patience available to him, as the young man praised Fyre and Thom's contributions to the group.

A rambling monologue segued without warning into tales of favorite concerts and Hollywood dreams while Thom smiled and nodded.

Even at inconvenient moments, he was never rude to the fans. Their devotion kept the lights on, kept him fed and comfortable. He once got through one of these exchanges while wrecked with the flu, staving off the urge to vomit until a girl outside of a pharmacy hugged him and walked away smelling her signed napkin. Meaning he had a few minutes to give to this dazzled young lad.

"I still play the keyboard and clarinet for the marching band, but when I pick up my bass I feel something entirely different. It's like the bass is the ground floor of the musical piece." Grocery Boy made a wave with his hand. "The...the..." He frowned, tapping his temple.

"Meaningful element of background." Thom pulled a pithy statement from an interview in hopes of wrapping this up. "You don't always notice it compared to vocals and lead guitar, but its absence leaves a noticeable wake."

"Genius," the kid whispered, his brown eyes misting. His Adam's apple bobbed as he swallowed. "I notice you. You're genius."

Thom's heart did swell in gratitude at that statement. Brian and Jonnie, the image men, got mobbed in public. As one of the only mega-famous black men currently working in rock, Jonas turned plenty of heads too. Thom typically only hit the radars of superfans, hardcore bass geeks, and horny women familiar with his reputation and eager to hop on the orgasmic thrill ride.

Moments like the current one reminded him that he mattered and possessed the ability to influence people's lives for the better. A blessing he didn't wish to squander.

He offered his hand in appreciation, and the kid shook vigorously, his palm damp. "Need me to sign anything?" Thom pulled him in for a half-hug and slap on the back.

The teen fan patted his pockets. "Crap. I left all my stuff in my locker. Do you have a pen?"

Thom began to shake his head when Megan reached in her purse and said, "Here," producing a marker.

He thanked her and signed the boy's apron before they parted ways and entered the store to fluorescent lighting and the musty smells of produce on the verge and cardboard, the wheels of his cart squeaking against linoleum. Over a crackly intercom, a man interrupted the din of an easy listening hit to announce that cleanup was needed on aisle four.

"I'm always labeling tapes and files." Megan's smile was wan as she picked up a red candle from a seasonal display, sniffed it, and set it down. "So I tend to have a marker on hand."

Thom took note of the table full of heart-shaped candy boxes, teddy bears, and flowers before angling the cart and turning down a center aisle.

Valentine's Day was afoot. He wouldn't be caught dead buying her any of this cheap, generic landfill fodder. She deserved jewelry or a vacation, and he'd damn sure dress her in the most scorching lingerie his millionaire's salary could pay for.

If they were still an item in a month, that was.

His insides twisted at the prospect of parting ways, and before his brain spent too much time on the painful subject, he redirected to where they'd been conversationally before he'd met the fan. "As you were saying, before the interruption? It's not that you don't want to tell me, but what?"

"Wow, you really are a good listener." Her tone surprised but not sarcastic, she set a jar of pickled jalapeño peppers in the cart.

"When I have to be or want to be, yes. Sharp memory as well. You're thinking breakfast burritos?"

"Tacos." She added a container of habanero salsa. "Extra spicy. And maybe some much-deserved margaritas?"

"Sold."

"Speaking of margaritas, I have a random question for you that applies to what we were talking about earlier."

"Of course."

A middle-ager in collegiate apparel shuffled past a shelf of boxed rice, and Thom looked down upon catching puzzled recognition in her eyes. He'd never get to have a meaningful conversation with Megan if today become Meet-and-Greet Tuesday.

"Does the name Mad Dog Margarita mean anything to

you?" A plastic-wrapped package of tortillas hit the metal basket with a subdued plunk, punctuating her straightforward query.

Memories of a music festival from a few years ago drifted up, nostalgic recollections of playing at nightfall to a sea of boozy fans, their tents sprinkling the grass behind them like assorted marbles. "Indeed. Not a name so much as a line from a song called "Dublin Blues." Singer's name was Guy Clark. Helluva a good man."

Thom sang a quick, throaty tribute to the singer, crooning sad, bluesy lyrics about rolling cigarettes and fighting off the shakes while lost to the grips of alcohol withdrawal.

"Was, as in he died?"

"May he rest in peace." Thom kissed his fingertips and lifted them skyward. He'd played some damn good poker during that festival. Trounced Brian for once.

They rounded the corner at the end of an aisle, coming up on refrigerated cases of dairy and eggs. Thom snagged two cartons of extra-large eggs, his taste for mischief activated.

"Can we just do meat and cheese?" With a slight frown directed at his eggs, Megan selected a package of shredded cheddar.

"These are for the post-meal entertainment." He rubbed his hands together like a scheming villain. Wait until she saw what he had in store—a dish best served cold. And runny.

"I'm never one to cast aspersions on creative sexytimes, but hard no to any activities that might put salmonella in my vagina."

A balding man wearing a double-denim outfit slashed Megan a crusty look as he passed with a cart full of dog food and toilet paper.

Megan countered the judgmental fellow with a big grin and wave.

Thom pulled her body to his, brushing his lips against her

temple. "I never defined the nature of the entertainment, so mind out of the gutter. Have I told you how much I like you yet?"

Massive understatement, but it didn't serve his end of getting closer to her by clinging too tightly or spilling his guts.

A soft look on her face, one he hadn't seen before, came through when she gazed up at him. He was half-tempted to whip out his phone and photograph that look, both to capture her striking beauty and to forever commemorate that time in the Podunk grocery store when she looked at him like he was the best man on earth.

Best not for his money or accomplishments, but for who he was inside.

"You've shown me." She kissed his cheek.

Trust tentatively established, he circled back to a delicate subject. "Why did you ask me about the mad dog margarita line?" He appraised rows of glistening poultry parts wrapped in plastic as they approached the meat. "Light meat or dark?"

"Boneless, skinless breast meat, please."

He picked out the freshest-looking cuts of what she wanted and ticked down the seconds, awaiting her answer to the question that wasn't about chicken.

She tapped her short nails on the handrail of the cart as if fidgeting ordered her thoughts or regulated her emotions. "That was the name of our anonymous sponsor, the one who funded the last investigation. The one where all the weird stuff happened. Usually, the investors with super deep pockets are celebrities, socialites, or royalty. In that order of possibility."

"And you hoped I might know them, or at least know of them? Have a clue as to who would pick that name?" He caressed the spot between her shoulders, willing his strokes to both assure her it was okay to open up and banish his anxiety that she merely kept him close in hopes of using him for clues to identify her benefactor.

"It was a long shot." She gave the cart a slight jerk when a wheel got stuck.

"Well, let's unpack the subtext of the song. Perhaps that will lead us somewhere." They strolled down a freezer aisle, and Thom scored two pints of strawberry ice cream, licking his lips as he stole a peek at Megan's lips. He did have designs on erotic food play later, just not with those eggs.

She nodded. "Good call."

"It's about a man with regrets and a lot of problems who is left alone with his longing." Thom swallowed past a lump in his throat. That track grazed a number of his own wounds, an odd synchronicity if there ever was one. He forged ahead before introspection stole his train of thought. "He's asking for forgiveness, both from his unrequited love and, as I understand it, from everyone he's hurt or wronged while careening through a selfish and unexamined life."

"Does he deserve forgiveness?" Her contemplative tone, finished with a savvy edge, introduced personalized dimensions that were impossible to miss.

He pursed his lips. "Probably not. But he asks anyway, because there's humility in the asking, even if the request is undeserved."

"Additional cashier to the front, additional cashier to the front."

The humdrum interruption would have been funny if not for how serious the atmosphere had grown. Thom's pulse bumped in fast beats now, his breath quick and his underarms warm as he used the song as both shield and vehicle.

Had he ever opened up to another person about his regrets, how he drew upon compulsive sex to salve his lack of love and inability to bond? Vulnerable and with his heart in his hands, here he was asking someone else to please see and accept him.

Did the egotistical, addictive defenses that he hid behind all stem from his parents' rejection of his life path, how he hungered for more human connection in the face of his superficial celebrity lifestyle? Was all he wanted, ultimately, a goddamn fucking *hug*?

He wiped a rogue tear from the corner of his eye. Why was Megan so quiet?

"I think there's also nobility in granting a request for forgiveness, even if the party in the position to give is skeptical of whether the asker has earned salvation," she finally said.

Good God, how many women's hearts had he torn asunder? How many of them had collapsed into piles of tears long after he'd jetted out of town, clinging to hopes that he'd call while facing up to the realization that he would not?

He'd burned through so many lovers. Watery images of their bodies, what little he'd catalogued of their faces, made up a documentary of sleaze. One after the other, in an obscene receiving line, they'd molded themselves into the pornographic characters they thought he wanted to see perform.

Before shame could pulverize him into an unrecognizable, gory mess, he spoke.

"Perhaps. Or maybe he should not have even asked. It's presumptuous of him, really, to make any more requests of others, when all he's done is take." Anger came through in his speech, a force directed inward with a heat he didn't yet know how to cool.

Her reaction look signaled that she'd gotten the underlying meaning. She made a noncommittal sound. "What about the margaritas, what do they mean?"

While they ambled to the checkout registers, all closed

except for a single cashier faced with a ten-cart line, Thom purged his angst with a cleansing breath. None of this was about him, a lesson he could stand to internalize. "Well, the man's an alcoholic trying to quit. The drinks represent what he wants to run back to, his weakness and vice. In the absence of that numbing medicine he craves, he's forced to look inside and confront what he sees."

"So his choice is to feed his addiction or go inward and face the fundamental source of the pain he feels in the absence of that drug."

"Precisely," Thom said through a dry mouth, stilling their cart behind an oblivious shopper lost in a tabloid.

"Ugh, the rabbit hole beckons." She ran a hand through her hair and stuttered a thin laugh.

He answered her chuckle with his own, thankful for the quenching water of her irreverence. "Elaborate?"

She faced him with furrowed brows. "Do you believe that everything happens for a reason? In a cosmic sense?"

Their cart inched forward as an elderly cashier with hot pink nails processed her deluge of customers.

He really ought to sit with questions like this more often. After all, he'd been cosmically blessed by the mysterious anointment of fame that millions craved but few obtained. "I suppose so, yes. No other way to account for my luck."

"Um, hello, your talent and hard work."

"Thank you, Megan." Felt good to thank another person for a compliment as opposed to replying with smug agreement or a conceited smirk. Baby steps.

Made him feel more like a human and less like an insecure, overinflated scoundrel, a shift that he could come to love. Because it meant he could truly love himself.

"So hear me out. This might sound nuts, but do you think this benefactor wanted us to find each other? That some intelligent force sent a string of events into motion, leading to us having this very conversation about some sad folk song?" she asked.

He loaded items on to the conveyor belt. Her hypothesis was a stretch, though he supposed that anything was possible. "Maybe. Though what's the benefactor's stake in you and me?"

"Unclear. It would help if I knew one thing about this benefactor. One fact to get me started on research."

"Can I ask why it all matters? What's driving your quest for answers?" Packaged food items slid down the black conveyor belt, the old woman ringing them up.

"I need to put all these pieces—the watch, the book, the possession, you, Mr. Shadow Creep returning—into some context or I'll go crazy. I need to feel as if I have control over my own life, even if it's full of weird paranormal stuff. I can't be a puppet, you know?"

"Fair." He set a bag of coffee on the moving slab of rubber and considered his next words. "You know one thing I've found, when creatively blocked and such, is that stepping away from a problem can be the exact thing required to find a solution. Gives the brain time to rest and recharge. Solutions to our big conundrums tend to come when we aren't actively fixated on them, as paradoxical as it sounds."

She knocked her hip into his and added a bottle of tequila and two cans of frozen orange juice to the moveable feast. "Sounds legit. But no more mansplaining."

"Alright," he laughed, duly chastised by her playful admonishment. "But does this mean we can at least have a break and enjoy our meal?"

"Absolutely." With a sly bit of eye contact, she introduced the ice cream into the mix. "Strawberry, eh?"

He leaned in to whisper in her ear. "Because you taste like strawberries. All of you."

"Bullshit. My pussy tastes like pussy. I've tasted it on other people's lips. Including yours."

The cashier snapped her head up, blushing and open-mouthed. She looked at Thom and stammered awkwardly, "You talk like Prince Charles."

Thom choked back a laugh to spare the poor old bird's feelings, though looking at Megan while he did so made his effort more challenging, as she mirrored him, her body convulsing with swallowed laughter.

I love you, Megan.

Egad. He swallowed that rather dangerous and potentially life-altering thought too.

SEVEN

MEGAN FILLED HER MOUTH WITH ANOTHER BITE OF SOFT warm heaven, chewy meat and tortilla offsetting the spicy sourness of taste-bud-puckering jalapeño. She washed her food down with a smoky-sweet drink of her frozen margarita and concentrated on the cold-on-hot contrast on her tongue instead of that damn song. Maybe Gary knew more than he let on. She'd call him later and feel things out. Better to worry about the paranormal predicament than what it might mean to enjoy a lazy brunch with her celebrity one-night stand.

"Are you from around here?" Thom asked, finishing the last of his food and sliding his plate across the table.

A kick of defensiveness made her suspect, albeit irrationally, that he was mocking her.

Her skittish thoughts wandered to the cracked tiles on her bathroom floor, blemishes she hadn't bothered to call maintenance about. A previously acceptable lack of living room drapes and the cigarette burn on her sofa now irritated her like a stone in the shoe.

Hosting a big rock star in her puny home underscored her

insignificance, thrusting their differences in stature and lifestyle to the forefront. What a foray into attempting to date again.

"New Denmark, born and raised." She threw her napkin on her plate, quashing the temptation to play with her leavings. "The closest semi-real city is Cedar Rapids. Ever heard of it?" The little bite to her question irritated her. Real subtle, Megan.

"I have." His brown eyes were kind and focused on her. "We actually played there in the nineties. Great crowd. They screamed the loudest of any room I remember that year. Funny, the things that stick in our minds."

She leaned back in her chair, her muscles loosening, curious to know more. Screw self-consciousness. She was who she was and had never been anyone else. Never tried or wanted to be, and he could take her or leave her. "Do you like touring?"

He picked up the saltshaker and set it down. "Yes and no. Being on the road is lots of fun but destabilizing. Life begins to feel surreal, unmoored, and just as you get used to it, it's time to go home. Which can be depressing, because you've gotta face reality while carrying around the remnants of what you did while lost in the funhouse of your surreal life. Kind of like being two people. I suppose that's why musicians like Jonas settle down early and remain faithful. Start families. To have that integrity of being one person, and someone they respect."

He smiled at her in a raw way that seemed to ask a question.

His smile cut her open. But as she sat with that discomfort, an awful realization emerged. They weren't quite in sync. A subtle skew, but one she felt acutely. When he advanced in this emotional way, her urge to retreat followed.

With everything else going on, she was too tired to examine her aversion. "I think that we can learn to love and respect ourselves without changing."

As if picking up on her deflection, his features hardened. A curt bob of his head followed, the responses of someone who didn't open up easily. "Do you have other brothers and sisters besides the one you shared the room with?"

Rationally, Megan knew that she wasn't the asshole here, but reason didn't help. They both knew that their dalliance was coming to an end, but they hadn't yet found a way to talk about it maturely. Time or necessity would soon negate this non-concept of them. "Four brothers. Two older, two younger. I think my parents would have forgotten that I existed if I wasn't committed to being noticed and clamoring for attention in any way I could. Explains a lot, I suppose."

"Like what?"

"My career path."

"The path to English professor was paved by a search for attention? I'm listening."

"I've been a drama kid since elementary school. I guess when I was onstage, I felt free. At liberty to be myself while playing a character, if that makes any sense. I could exhibit myself *and* hide. And the applause at the end became addictive. In high school, I stared getting typecast as the seductive, slutty Lady Macbeths and home-wrecking jezebels and whatnot, but that kind of attention worked for me too. I had red hair, big boobs, and a wild side, and I just kind of slid into the script society had written for me." She shook her head as teenage memories flooded back. A boy had enjoyed her body and betrayed her afterward in one of those drama rooms. Girls wrote obscene notes about her in the bathroom stalls for the rest of the year. "And sirens, how could I forget? I played three sirens."

He leaned forward, the look in his eyes tender and soft. "I feel so connected to you right now. Everything you said about the stage and playing a persona is spot on for me."

Unprocessed emotions hammered Megan in a ferocious bombardment. A flaying pain travelled from her legs to her neck. Why was Thom toying with her feelings like this? She was supposed to be dead inside, impervious to any more heartbreak, but he insisted on taking a mallet to her hardness.

Her hands trembled as she collected his plate before he could reply, stacking his atop hers, pathetically moved by the sight of his leftovers. He was a person like any other, one who left a sole remaining bite of taco on the plate. She liked sharing special moments with him.

She hadn't even made it to the sink before water started wobbling in her vision.

Legs shaky, she stood and took the tableware to the basin, the edge of one dish bumping into a wine glass that split in half on impact.

"Fuck." A knot of anger twisted inside her chest as she clutched the edge of the sink, rage boomeranging to set off white-hot reverberations inside.

Here she was, in her crappy apartment, all messed up over a rock star—and not for the first time. Breaking dishes and remembering that she drank alone, unemployed. She just couldn't manage to live her life right.

"Hey, hey." His strong arms circled her, and he rocked gently. "What happened? Did you cut yourself?"

Somehow, the concerned question made it all worse. Because he didn't love her. Not really. No one ever had. Megan was the wild ho with the tongue barbells who guys used to sow their wild oats before bringing that nice kindergarten teacher home to mama.

"Yeah," she snorted, spackling on sarcasm with a trowel. "I cut myself. Then I did it again and again and again. Except instead of scars on my wrists, I have them on the inside." Megan used a bitter laugh to mock herself and wiped her eyes with the back of her hand. "That was some middle school emo girl poetry garbage right there, huh?"

"Your point wasn't garbage, it was profound. And the last thing I want is to hurt you more than you've already been hurt by men like me. I hope you know that."

She turned around and planted two hands in the middle of his solid chest, a gentle push creating some space between them. A berth to breathe, as if she could think more clearly in those fifteen inches and better resist the lure to fade into him. "So what do you want?"

A pause of several eternal seconds had her awaiting his answer with an infuriating eagerness. She didn't have the power anymore, that hard dignity she wore like armor. Her wall had fallen, yet she kept up floundering appearances of having a fortress to hide within.

"I don't know." God, his words expanded to fill the room in the same way that he did. Larger than life, leveling impact with every syllable or step. "Because it's not something I've wanted ever before with anyone else. But I want to go to the grocery store with you and buy chicken and salsa. I want to drive around town with you and have you show me around all your old haunts. I want to meet your parents."

She allowed her tears to come, and wet rivulets streaked her cheeks. Her folks had given up on her long ago and surrendered their fantasy of a sweet daughter in a white dress walking past pews stocked with admiring guests as she marched to meet her groom. They'd said bye-bye to her along with their daydream of a wedding day with blush on Megan's cheeks, her hymen intact, and Jesus looking down in approval from his station on the crucifix.

At least Mama and Papa had a bevy of grandchildren to

stuff in their minivan thanks to her brothers and their untattooed, demure, God-fearing wives.

"I feel like you're teasing me into thinking there's the possibility of a chance." She pressed her lips into his shoulders, muffling her words, like that would make the impact hurt less.

His strokes moved up and down her spine, assuring and steadfast, a hand roaming to her hair and massaging her scalp. How easy he made it to melt, fade, forget. "Why would you think I'm teasing you?"

"Relationships just haven't worked for me. I'm cursed in that area of life. I can't fit myself into that box, you know? I suck at being the kind of woman that men want to be with long-term." Eventually she gave up, or maybe cut a deal, depending on how you looked at it.

Megan got accustomed to using them like they used her. She strode out of bedrooms before her lovers had a chance to reject her.

"I'm not those men. I'm me, and I want to be with you long-term."

What a concept, after all these years. She hadn't tried to make a serious relationship stick since her mid-twenties. And of course, she'd tried too hard, overcompensated, and driven the guy away. And her checkered past—and, hell, present and future—wasn't limited to a dicey dating track record. "I lost my steady job. I'm a mess."

"Your schedule's flexible. Meaning you could join me on the tour. If you'd like."

"You have a pretty good idea of my storied sexual history."

"We've covered that ground. Next."

"I hear voices, and they led me to a bizarre arcane book that I have to figure out what to do with. My oldest friend is a shadow monster that lurks at the edge of my bed, and there may even be bodysnatching and possession in the mix. I'm not right, Thom."

He looked her dead in the eye, his face stern with conviction. "Can I level with you?"

For someone rumored to be one of the most notorious players on the celebrity scene, Thom sure had a no-nonsense way about him. Quite a treat, after dealing with her fair share of manipulators and pick-up artists with a taste for gaslighting and other forms of messing with women's minds. "Always."

"I want to be with you. Serious, exclusive, monogamous, whatever you wish to call it. If that's not what you want, or you aren't sure, I can live with that. I'll meet you wherever you are, and if that place involves us parting company in short order, then so be it. I won't put pressure on you, and I'm prepared to accept an outcome that I'd rather not see come to pass, but now you know where I stand." He took one of her hands in his larger one and pressed her palm to his chest, firm enough so she could feel the thump of his life force. "Now you know what's in here. For you."

In the span of *one day*, her life had flipped upside down. Yes, she had feelings for Thom, and they kept on growing. She liked him and could relax around him. He made her laugh and feel good about herself. She respected and admired him.

Still, moving fast was moving fast, and Megan was not used to fast movement in this particular direction. With all the other madness unspooling around her, someone had to be the brake and slow the roll of this wild and crazy insta love train. "I need time. I hope you understand."

He might have flinched, but if he did, he masked the wince with a neutral expression before she could feel bad for disappointing him. "Of course. Now how about a palate cleanser?"

"In what sense?"

"Grab those eggs from the fridge."

She grinned, reenergized by the return of an unsolved mystery promising mischief.

◊

"WHAT'S THE DEPARTMENT CHAIR'S ADDRESS?" THOM ASKED with a casual calmness from the passenger seat, tapping his phone screen.

Stone cold. She nearly squeed.

"I can't," Megan hissed, though chemical streaks coursed through her system when she glanced in the backseat, gaze falling upon two cardboard packages of slimy, self-contained goop bombs. "He'll know it was me."

"So? You've already been terminated."

"True." She snuck another peek at the egg cartons, each one arranged innocently in the middle seat, as the high preceding the commission of a forbidden act changed into a purer collection of positive emotions. Yes, their impending revenge was juvenile and not high-minded. But so what. Thom had been thinking about her, upset on her behalf. He cared enough to want to right a wrong done against her, and that was what counted. "You're so weirdly gallant, Thom James. And I can't believe you've been plotting all this time. That's diabolical."

"He deserves worse. We can't keep driving in circles. Address. Please."

She giggled and did a little shimmy in her seat, the fun of this risky excursion blotting out unpalatable memories of afternoons and nights spent at the address in question. "1402 Golden Terrace Drive."

"Good grief." He rolled his eyes, plugging info into his cell. "Sounds like somewhere a serial killer would keep bodies stashed under the floorboards."

The giddy trill of her laughter escalated to a full-on

cackle, and warmth spread over her chest in a sweep. Thom never ceased to find ways to amuse her or surprise her with his arsenal of endearing disarmaments. "How the hell did you come up with that?"

"I don't know, I can just imagine a Netflix narrator saying, 'The atrocities occurred here, at the sleepy residence of 1402 Golden Terrace Drive'."

The booming narrator voice he affected, over the top in his English accent combined with the randomness of this madness, had her laughing so hard her sides hurt. "Stop."

"Concentrate, concentrate. We're coming up on the target. Turn left. Now, now."

She drove up to a four-way stop and jerked the wheel, snickering when the tires squealed.

She was practically popping a wheelie in broad daylight on the humble streets of New Denmark. What would all the nice church ladies think if they saw her, the town whore, taking her badness to a new low? Therapeutic laughter continued to roll out of her throat. "Calm. Focus. Head in the game."

"That's a hideous house," Thom said as Megan slowed in front of the chair's split-level.

"No shit. He'd lay in bed and talk at me about his remodeling plans until he fell asleep."

Thom made a face like he'd drank sour milk. "It keeps getting worse. Should I kill him?"

Before she could crack a joke, Megan caught sight of a second car in the driveway, parked alongside the chair's two-door Ford. Her skin pulled tight as she placed where she'd seen the pink Volkswagen bug with the Iowa Hawkeyes bumper sticker: in the student parking lot.

The little jellybean belonged to Hailey Winters—and eighteen-year-old Stillwater English major who'd lamented the other week that she'd do *anything* to pass Literature and Culture of the Renaissance.

"Noooo," Megan said.

"What?"

"He's screwing an undergrad now. That's her car."

"You're positive that's why she's here?"

She slipped him a knowing side-eye. "You should have seen how he leered at the visiting high school recruits."

"On that note, shall we get started?"

Megan composed herself with a silent goodbye to Stillwater. Let adjuncts have her spring semester classes. She didn't owe that school another ounce of her time and labor, and a few more months of pay wasn't worth having to face those people again.

She snatched a carton from the front seat and jumped out, Thom joining her on the sidewalk with his own ammunition.

"Let he who is without sin cast the first stone." Immediately after speaking, he frowned and touched his lips.

"Yeah, not exactly the expression we're looking for, but it does have a nice ring. On the count of three?"

Thom popped his lid and threw an egg in the air, catching it so delicately that it didn't shatter.

A curl of warmth threaded through her lower half. An odd, random thing to get turned on by, though she figured his move symbolized his devotion while showing off his remarkable grace and dexterity. Made him look cool, and loyal.

"One." Megan filled her hand with a smooth orb, enjoying the texture of sloppy destruction wrapped in a flimsy shell.

"Two." Thom held the egg over his eye, the weirdness making her laugh again.

"Three." Her heart leapt, and she unloaded, the first

projectile nailing the department chair's living room window with a hearty crack.

A super-satisfying trail of yellow slime bled down glass, and soon she was lost to the moment, swearing under her breath as eggs pelted his front door, driveway, and mailbox until it looked like a giant had used the house in lieu of a tissue.

The door opened a crack. "Hey!" the chair yelled in a panicked, high-pitched version of his normal voice, the vocal alteration an awkward and cringe-worthy novelty.

"Shit," she squealed, grabbing Thom, who was reared back like a baseball player preparing to pitch.

Before they could flee to the getaway car, an awful sight stopped her dead: the chair was butt-naked except for a pair of black socks and a blue condom sheathing his half-hard dick.

He began to jog down the walkway in a clumsy trot, making footprints in the snow as he shouted, "I'm gonna sue you for property damages, O'Neil! Ruin your ass! You'll never teach or publish again! The only academic work you'll be able to find is sucking cock in the athletic department's locker rooms, you cheap whore—"

Out of the corner of her eye, she saw Thom's arm wind up and fling. His shot landed in a hard and direct hit to the target's face. The chair stood there, stunned and nude, with glop the color of sickly snot hanging from his chin and nose. He picked shell off his upper lip and spat.

"Apologize," Thom said calmly. "Apologize to Megan for ruining her livelihood, and how you spoke to her just now."

Poor little Hailey, clad in a bra and underwear, appeared in the doorway. "What's going on? Dr. O'Neil?"

"You deserve better, Hailey," Megan said. "You deserve a real mentor. You don't need creeps like this to get ahead. I promise."

Hailey made a puzzled face, scurried back inside, and returned a moment later to dash across the lawn with her clothes and purse in her arms. The pink bug peeled off.

The chair clasped his hands over his junk in the fig leaf position, gaping at Thom. "Aren't you on television?"

An egg nailed him right between the eyes, exploding in a blast of yolk. "Apologize."

"Quit throwing eggs at me," he whined, flinging glop off his face.

"You know how to make the pain stop." Thom held up a third grenade, the weapon pinched between thumb and forefinger.

"Sorry," he muttered, moving one hand to shield his head.

"Not good enough." Thom juggled the egg. A muffled buzz that he ignored sounded off near the back pocket of his jeans. "To whom are you sorry, for what, and why?"

The chair let off a low growl and glared at Megan. "I'm sorry, Megan, for denying your tenure application, and for standing back while the others went after you. I'm sorry I didn't do more to stand up for you and protect you when everyone got upset about our affair. I threw you under the bus because it was easier for me, and that was wrong."

Egg number three sailed through the air and struck him on the temple. "That's *Dr.* O'Neil to you." Thom's phone rang.

"Sorry, Dr. O'Neil," the chair gritted out while Thom's cell chirped with a notification.

"Is that acceptable, Megan?" Thom asked.

She told the chair, "Okay. Sure. And just so you're aware, I plan to reach out to Hailey and make sure you didn't cross any lines. Quid pro quo sexual harassment against a student is a serious offense. So don't get any ideas about calling the cops today unless you want me to expedite my pro bono investigation."

The chair paled to an ashy hue and winced before Megan turned away from him. She and Thom walked to the car, his phone continuing to make noise.

"You're sure you don't need to get that?" she asked when the ringtone warned of yet another incoming call.

EIGHT

Conventional wisdom holds that people don't change much after a certain age. They may develop new hobbies and interests, sure, or even learn to see situations and circumstances from different perspectives if prompted by some life-altering event. Behavior patterns might shift, motivated mostly by personal incentive.

Core personalities, though, remain set. The deeper stuff, doubly so. Morals and values. Notions of right and wrong. One's capacity for remorse, regret, and introspection.

In the moment, in Megan's arms while glorious buttery sunshine streamed through her bedroom windows to glaze their tangle of nude flesh, Thom called bullshit. With her, a hidden part of him had come to life. Whether he'd starved it, or ignored it, or if it had never existed at all until he met her, he could not say with certainty. But it was here now. He'd found a missing treasure he'd never known he'd lost.

"What are you thinking about?" Her breath grazed his cheek, as warm as her skin.

"Just you." He memorized her with his fingertips, making a study of her jawline, eyebrows, the groove above her upper lip. Three brown moles dotted the side of her neck, and he kissed each one before continuing his exploration to the sides of her breasts. "How stunning you are. How special."

His throat clogged with unspoken emotion, a sudden tenderness afflicting his nose and eyes. Would they part ways soon, out of geography and necessity? Someone kept calling him, Brian or their manager, and he couldn't leave his phone on silent forever. If he reneged on his duties and obligations, a lot of people would suffer disappointment and even loss of livelihood.

Unfair to hold others' lives hostage to his whims—even if he was falling in love for the first time.

"You're leaving, aren't you?" He'd never heard her speak in that tone before, unguarded and a note or two lower than usual, and it lodged a spear in his heart. If only they'd met some other time, some other way.

He owed her transparency, at least. The truth at every step, no platitudes or sugarcoating. He adjusted his position, scooting down and propping himself up on one elbow to bring them face to face. Fuck, those green eyes were staring back at him. He wanted to wake up every morning like this, gazing at Megan bathed in sunlight. The glow made a golden halo around her head and threaded ribbons of light into her fiery waves. His angel. His fire goddess.

"Looks that way. Someone keeps calling, and the tour runs for six more weeks." He spiraled her hair through his fingers, cataloging the exact texture to memory. "This doesn't have to mean goodbye. Why don't you pack up and come along?"

She traced aimless shapes on his outer arm as if putting her thoughts into motion. "I don't know. I'd feel like a hanger-on. Would everyone be giving me side eye, annoyed that there's this random groupie tagging along for the rest of the tour?"

He really didn't care about anyone's opinions of Megan to

be honest. Fyre and their staff had stirred plenty of far more dubious hangers-on into the mix over the years.

A couple of summers ago, Jonnie had taken a shine to a pensive German mystery author who cropped up on the European leg of the tour and never left. The man ate and drank far more than his lithe form would suggest, his robust consumption costing the Fyre operation a solid four figures along the way.

Thom thought the hungry German was there to stay, especially when the possibility of a marriage proposal was broached over the band's poker table. But the novelist's husband crashed a party in Philly a few days later, out of his mind and bawling apologies for some midlevel marital infraction. The German devoured Jonnie's heart as his last meal before heading home.

Jonnie was crushed beyond recognition, and a barrage of informal therapy sessions at the hands of Thom, Jonas, and Brian followed. Despite their best efforts, Jonnie slid into catatonic depression, and the summer mega-tour folded a month early. The rhythm guitarist had since sworn off men, and Thom occasionally harbored lingering fantasies of suing that damn author for damages. His books sucked too.

Long story short, Thom had accrued some band capital. His mates would have to warmly welcome Megan and not bitch about her presence. No exceptions. "Everyone will love you." He kissed the tip of her nose like he liked to do. "Have you met anyone besides me? I guess you must have, since you got invited to that party where we met."

He braced himself for hearing about who else she'd been with, though he didn't judge or even care anymore. After all, he had her now.

"I was kind of casually seeing that new roadie Ryan, mostly just to get to you. I'm not proud of that. I know that using people is shitty. Other than him, I was on a first name basis with some of the other crew. I'm sure it would be cool to meet Brian and Jonas and Jonnie." She went quiet. Sighed.

A light inside of him flickered out. The sunshine no longer felt as heavenly warm. "But? I hear the but."

"I'm just in a really weird place right now, as you know. I feel like I need to slow down and reflect. Figure out what's next for me. Starting with the book." She walked her fingers up and down his hirsute chest. "I think if I kicked off and followed your band around, I'd feel irresponsible, you know? Like I was running from myself."

"You wouldn't be following. You make it sound as if you'd be a burden, but you wouldn't be. And if it's work you want, we could find you work. I'm sure we could hustle up paranormal investigation jobs on the road. Haunted roadside attractions or whatever. We'll build you a good website."

The smile this thought pulled from her was sad. "That's really specific. Thank you for thinking of me."

The ache in his throat returned, tingling with pressure. "Now it sounds like you're the one leaving and saying goodbye."

"I'm here now, aren't I?" Her voice grew seductive again, that smoky vixen's drawl he'd die trying to resist.

"You are. And I'm glad." The touch of her buttercream skin, electric, excited him. In seconds his dick was stiff, but instead of caving, he breathed steadily until some nourishment flowed upward to his brain. "But I want you to know this isn't just about sex, or fun. I have feelings for you, real ones. I want this to work out. I want us to work out."

"For that to be a possibility, I think we need to take things slow. One step at a time."

He laughed with affection and cupped her breasts. "We're currently naked in bed. Hardly taking things slow."

"Yeah, true, but that part never was slow to begin with."

Mesmerized by her, he fell into the thrall of a sensual flow and surrendered to the moment. He'd show her with his body, with his lovemaking, how much he cared. Give her more than words. "This part can be slow."

She reached out and touched his cheek, a lingering caress touched with the pain of impending separation, and rolled to her back.

Thom never broke eye contact as he shifted his weight on top of her. Let her see the moisture in his eyes, how much she meant to him. Their dance commenced in silence, physical pleasure assuming a secondary role to the symphony of emotions their bodies sang.

"Megan." He brushed his lips to hers, a graze to feel the softness of her parted mouth, and savored her breath.

When she yielded, pliant beneath him, he slipped into her and melted. They moved together, silent save for the music of their emotions and the dance of bodies as one. His hands were in her hair, hers on his back. The midday sun blessed them from beyond window glass, their cocoon, their bed offering protection from the winter cold beyond.

He saw colors suddenly, grasped little bits of their surroundings in impressions more profound than the details would suggest. A poster on her wall, gilt frame casing a playbill with words in Italian and blue velvet dresses. The air smelled of her perfume and their bodies.

Without utterance, he spoke love with his body, moving into and out of her with languid strokes. Touching her. Feeling her. Remembering her.

As their temples brushed, a few wet drops from his eye lubricated the passage of skin on skin, as above so below. "Don't leave me, Megan."

"I'm right here." She looped her legs around his hips and her arms around his shoulders, enveloping him, her body as sacred as any shrine. "I'm here now."

Thom did his best to abide the power of now, to live in

the moment without expectation or anticipation, to drink what he had without thirsting for more. Near impossible, when the only thing he wanted in the world was more Megan. More closeness, more contact, more union of their two hearts.

For the first time, he'd forgotten about any sort of endgame of sex, disregarded a prior obsession with securing his own payoff, while abandoned to her.

He only remembered the ultimate goal when she moaned and arched, her walls clenching as she bounced her hips in time with the contractions. That he knew the distinctive sound of her climax now shattered him. Would some other person hear it in the near future?

Her clamp on his shoulders relentless, she tensed to rigidity before collapsing limp.

With a few more strokes, he finished silently, the euphoria of release secondary to the maelstrom higher up in his body. Some hurricane of melodies churned, erstwhile foreign energies of a mysterious nature that he lacked the vocabulary to name. As tension left his body, he lowered from his elbows and faded into her, their tender bellies pressed together.

Once the magic drifted off to the unseen spiritual place it came from, leaving them as two human beings nude and smashed together in bed, he slid off her and to his side.

Content as a lazy cat, he stroked the curve running from her chest to her hip. He thought of a few things to say but nixed them all, deeming each one inadequate to capture his truth.

Tell me that isn't the last time. Lie to me. I promise, I'll believe. Lie to me for my own sake, just please don't leave.

"Where are you off to next?" She nibbled his ear. "That was phenomenal by the way. Though I don't need to tell you again with my words."

"I'll always accept feedback and suggestions for

improvement." He watched her out of the corner of his eye, pulling her to settle in the crook of his arm.

Bit of a test, that first statement. To float the idea of a next time and assess her reaction.

"You're golden." A pleasure sound accompanied her hard-to-read statement. "Now dazzle me with stories of the road, vagabond rocker. Where will you ramble to next on your big tour?"

That subject piqued his anxiety while souring his bliss. He'd rather entertain the notion of their relationship deepening than evoke subject matter that inevitably steered his mind into the vicinity of all those missed calls. "Omaha, I think," he said on a weighty sigh. "Though I ought to check and make sure."

"Go ahead." She trailed a sequence of flirty kisses from his cheek to his hairline. "I'm going to jump in the shower. Maybe we can go ice skating after, if you still want to?"

The fact that she remembered and still wanted to do the activity catapulted him out of his broody state.

"I'd love to." He burned with the urge to utter a similar phrase, one that nearly rhymed, but the timing was wrong. But hey, if he'd managed to finally learn how to make love, he could learn patience. He patted her bottom. "Godspeed. We'll reconvene once you're all cleaned up."

"Are you as good on the ice as you are in bed?" She sauntered to her bathroom.

"Nope. Absolute novice. You can teach me. Or mock me. Depending on your mood."

She laughed her radiant, harmonious, full-throat laugh. "I'll keep you on your toes guessing. Make yourself at home. I think there's a beer in the fridge, and I also have a bunch of different teas." Off she went, and water ran.

While Megan sang a few bars of the Guy Clark song adorably off-key from her station in the shower, Thom hopped into his jeans and went to her living room. He cocooned himself in the pleasure of his thoughts for a moment before turning to the unpleasant task of dealing with the phone calls and, he bet, confirming his suspicions. Before facing the probable wrath of Brian, he dawdled with fuzzy memories of making love to Megan for a spell.

Even the words themselves, *making love*, knocked him flat. He hadn't done that before, but he rather liked the slow play. If someone told him years ago that sex could be so much more than physical release, perhaps he would have changed his tune early on.

But he was grateful for how it all worked out because it meant he got to experience his emotional awakening with Megan. A woman worth making *his*, if she'd have him. The first step was to get her on the tour.

His chest dropped a notch. Speaking of tours and his band, time to face the music. He turned his phone on with the push of a button, swiped his finger across the screen, and checked the source of all those angry orange notifications.

Sure enough, Brian's name glowered at him, the string of letters practically vibrating with aggravation. Thom grimaced at the damage. "Bollocks."

He rang the front man, who answered after one beat of the dial tone. "Where the hell are you, off the grid? Been trying to reach you for twenty-four hours."

Thom flipped a few pages of Megan's wall calendar, curious about her routine. Was she regimented or casual, organized or spontaneous? His money was on spontaneous. "Popped out of town for a couple of days. Why are your knickers in a twist? The next show's not until Friday."

Brian had always been uptight, though lately he'd been wound tighter than usual, more obsessive and exacting. Thom suspected the chaos of the man's newly finalized divorce played a role in his doubling down on band matters, an area where he wielded a particular zest for control.

"You missed an interview," he responded crisply, true to form. "And flaky does not look good on us, mate. Ticket sales haven't been up to snuff, and we don't have an inch of leeway with the label right now."

One of Brian's less admirable qualities was his tendency to kowtow to label suits and other authority figures. To be fair, someone had to keep the gears of capitalism lubricated, and Brian was the bloke best qualified to grease the machine. Fyre had nowhere to go but down at this point, and Brian's knack for staving off the inevitable had legitimate merits of the monetary persuasion.

Thom was grateful that the company man role didn't fall to him. Just to take the piss, though, he threw out, "The label, the label. Buy buy buy, sell sell sell. You need to get laid."

Brian had always been the most monkish of the four, hadn't touched a groupie in years, but his failed marriage had turned him downright puritanical. Thom suspected that all of those unreleased loads festering in his sac had mutated into stress hormones.

"Oh, really?" Brian said in a smug, frustrated tone. "That's your solution to every one of life's challenges, isn't it? Shagging and blowjobs? Because that's what you're doing right now, I'm sure. Running off to dip your wick at the expense of all our careers. I swear, sex is all you ever think about."

Thom laughed at the bluster, though a knot of tension interwoven with embarrassment tightened in his midsection. It had been irresponsible and childish to vanish from St. Louis without a word, leaving the others worrying if he'd snapped and abandoned the tour. Journeymen rock stars had pulled weirder and more erratic stunts near the twilight of their careers, so Brian's distress wasn't necessarily irrational.

"Look, I'm just taking the piss. I apologize for the disappearing act, sincerely. You aren't wrong to get annoyed. I'm going to lay it all out there."

"Alright." Brian's tone calmed to its natural register, sleek and posh with steel angles, like James Bond's gun. "Please do."

"I met someone. A groupie I was with in St. Louis. I like her, I really like her, and I'm taking this seriously."

Brian snorted. "What?"

The front man better not say anything rude or derogatory about Megan. Brian never put down women, but he was rankled, so Thom had his guard up just in case. "What do you mean what? Is the notion that I would develop a romantic interest in one of the groupies unfathomably absurd to you?"

"The notion that you would develop a romantic interest in anyone beyond a few nights has me reeling. Where is this coming from? Did some major upheaval happen in your life, a disruption you aren't telling me about?"

Thom rubbed his ear. Brian had a point with the first sentence. "No, I'm not going through a midlife crisis or weathering a shock so severe it forced me to introspect for once. This just sort of happened. I can't explain it either, but we click, you know? We're relaxed around each other. Easy, and free to be ourselves. I've never experienced this, so I don't want to throw it away without making a real go of things."

A door shut, negating a din of background chatter. Brian said, "I'm happy for you, I am. And if you want to try and make it work with this woman, I'll support you and her in any way I'm able."

And wait for the "but" in five, four, three—

"But I need you in Omaha tomorrow morning."

Thom winced, his stomach sinking. "Why so early? The show isn't until Friday."

Brian huffed theatrically. "Wednesday, Thom, the show is Wednesday. As in the day after tomorrow."

He glanced back at the bedroom, his mind turning into a grimly ticking clock. "So I'll be in Omaha on Wednesday afternoon."

"No, because on Tuesday we have the dinner and drinks with those radio show contest winners."

Thom groaned as loud as he could. He'd forgotten about that chore. The last thing he wanted to do was say goodbye to Megan a day early to go make small talk with a table full of random people who all happened to be caller number seven. "Come on, man, I won't be missed."

"Absenteeism is awful optics and sends the wrong message. They'll assume you don't care."

"They'll be right."

"Thom. Stop. The last thing we want this year is to soil our image. Chariotz of Fyre is down to earth. Chariotz of Fyre loves our fans and is friendly and never rude. Chariotz of Fyre is grateful. Chariotz of Fyre is—"

"Alright, alright, message received. Christ, mate, listen to yourself. You sound like a coked-up Walmart manager trying to rally the troops on morale day."

"I'm having a staffer put you on the first flight to Omaha in the morning. Where are you right now?"

He rolled his eyes. Brian Shepherd and his one-track, tunnel-vision mind. Maybe Brian would be lucky enough to meet an ideal woman of his own one day. A woman skilled in the delicate, specialized surgery necessary to pull the stick out of his arse. "Cedar Rapids, Iowa."

"Great. Be at the airport at six. You know the drill from there."

Deplane, sail through yet another airport past turning heads and oohs of recognition, find one of Fyre's signature white Lexus couriers in the transportation area. Then off to go through the motions, again and again.

After a day spent blazing a path through a whole new worldview, the monotony of boomeranging back to the grind did not entice him in the slightest.

The prospect of free, willing women who existed for his sexual entertainment? The quintessential rock star job perk that once made the drudgery of the road all worth it? About as appealing as sticking his prick in a pencil eraser. "Yeah. Whatever."

Apparently satisfied, Brian hung up.

Rather than wasting a single second more of his precious time, Thom returned to the bedroom. He found Megan sitting on the bed flipping through her big book, one towel swaddling her body and a mismatched one wrenched into a knot around her wet hair. He swept his love into his arms.

Not a second to squander now. Not one.

NINE

IF SHE EXCELLED AT SWITCHING HEADSPACES EASILY, Megan would have pushed the book onto the floor and surrendered to Thom's kisses. In the fantasy that unfolded, she arched her neck to give him better access as she shimmied out of her towel. But the book won this round.

Her focus had zeroed onto an exciting tidbit. A lead that took shape when singing in the shower made her feel woozy and lightheaded, spaced out as if she shared her consciousness with another being. No coincidence. Especially considering the particular tune she'd belted, the one that'd burrowed into her ear earlier and refused to exit.

"Look at this." She moved the watch over the page she'd found the time piece bookmarking the other night. As her talisman slid across a cluster of sigils, the bundle of gears in the sixth circle turned. "This means...I don't know what. But fuck, I can almost taste it."

Thom shifted his weight to sit beside her. "Not to be presumptuous, but is this, perhaps, best left alone?"

"That's a logical point, but I'm inclined to say no. The book and watch worked on their own while we slept at the orphanage, so who's to say they won't revisit their conspiracy?"

"Conspiracy to what?" He ran his finger down the page, his other hand coming to rest on the small of her back.

"My working theory is that, at minimum, an entity or entities are using the book in efforts to escape the watch. The shadow being and maybe more want out."

"To what end?"

"I'm not sure. But people are in on it. Maybe Gary. Check this out." Holding the watch to hover above inked parchment, she sang a few lines of "Dublin Blues."

The gears in circle six picked up their pace, and the ones in number four joined. She moved thick stacks of pages, returning to the table of contents. "Section four is fire, and the logo for fire matches the insignia on the inside flap. So this is the fire book, whatever that means. Which we knew."

Thom hummed and rubbed his chin. "Okay. So what you're saying is that the song has a particular significance to the situation with the watch and the book, by way of the benefactor's name."

"Exactly. Mad Dog Margarita." She searched her memory for any useful nugget and came up short. "But who are they? What do they want?"

"Beats me. Maybe Gary will spill."

Synapses in her brain fired in a rapid rate. "He's a black box. I have a through line connecting me, this book, demons, and my watch. But what I can't get my head around is why I matter to this equation. I mean, anyone could sing this song. Not like I have a special connection to it."

"No." Thom's cadence was contemplative, revealing unspoken thoughts, and she listened. "But through the song, you have a connection to me. You said the first day we were together that there was dark energy around my band. I'm no paranormal expert, so this is me grasping at straws, but my guess is that your emotions are valuable in some way. That whoever is running this operation needs your unique connection to the shadow and whatever else."

Frustration thrummed, an agitated wave pulsing right beneath her surface, out of reach. She chewed the corner of her lip. "Okay, so here's a theory. The song is an incantation, and I'm the person who has to recite it. I still can't see why. Am I a vessel, or powerful? Do I go along with this or try to resist? I don't know what my best interests are."

Thom spoke after a pregnant pause. "Why don't we stop by Gary's later? It's clear that my presence disarms him. So I'll keep him off-balance and distracted while you poke around for what he might know."

She closed the book, appreciation for Thom replacing anxiety over the paranormal mystery and general spookiness. She'd never dated—or whatever they were labeling this—a man so loyal and patient. Maybe a long-distance relationship was feasible. In the past, she hadn't cared enough to try one, but the idea of letting Thom go without effort filled her with reluctance and mild depression. "Who called while I was showering?"

Against her body, his muscles tensed. "Brian. I have to leave in the morning."

A kick of pain struck her erstwhile indestructible emotional defenses, and she slouched. The bad news settled in like a splinter. "Oh. I thought we had until Friday to hang out."

"Me too. I'm sorry. I'm afraid the man will have a stroke, though, if I buck the tour schedule anymore." He wound a tendril of her hair around his finger, stroking her bare shoulder as he let go of the wavy sliver. "And as much as I'd love to stay, I do have responsibilities. People whose incomes depend on me honoring my commitments. I'm sorry, Megan, to spring this on you."

She picked at a frayed spot on her towel as an ache lodged deep in her chest. "I get it. Don't apologize."

"My offer still stands, just so you know. I won't pressure you, but you're welcome to come visit any time. Airfare's on me."

Her earlier points all still stood too, as much as she was growing to despise their circumstances. "I wish the timing sucked less."

"Same," he said with sincerity. "On that note, shall we go hit the ice?"

He knew their time together was limited and didn't want to spend it moping. A bittersweet acknowledgement and totally understandable. "I'd love to."

While she rose, he rubbed his knees and looked at his hands. She stood before him, her breath catching as she waited for him to speak, anticipating a big point she sensed was about to roll in like thunder.

"Megan?" He spoke her name with such tenderness, as if giving himself over to a higher presence, that all she could do was look him square in the eye. His soul rose from those artistic brown pools, issuing through windows of a life fully lived and perhaps only recently examined.

Examined thoroughly, though, and with the benefit of his formidable intellect and dedication. Though Megan gazed down at Thom—he was seated, and she was on her feet—she looked up to him more than she ever had another person.

"Yeah?" She failed to pitch her voice above a whisper, though it was the kind of whisper that stopped time.

"I've fallen in love with you. I don't say this to be manipulative or make demands, but I want you to know. And take it for what it's worth. I don't expect an answer. All I ask is that you find a moment to sit with my truth. That moment doesn't have to be right now."

If any other guy pulled this, dropping a bombshell the day

before he rambled off to rejoin his band, she would have been furious. Maybe even laughed in his face or told him to fuck right off with that emotional blackmail noise. But this was Thom, and she trusted him. She got him.

Whether she returned his sentiment, well, she didn't have a clear answer. She enjoyed him. Respected him. Cared about him, and genuinely wanted him to make the best choices for his own well-being, even if that meant leaving. She not only liked him, but she liked herself better when she was with him.

Was that love? Though she didn't want to sell her own feelings short, she desired even less to make a hasty leap and risk breaking his heart.

She hazarded the best, most frank response available, "I have feelings for you, too, big ones. I'm not sure what they mean yet. In part because I need time and space to think. Sort out...everything." Her gaze fell to the book, activating another round of speculation about its mysteries. "My kingdom for a moment of down time. To focus on one single thing. Like us, and our whirlwind romance. Or this paranormal situation. One at a time, you know?"

"I get it." There was resignation in his answer, an understated sadness that in turn made her sad. And had her wondering if she was the asshole here. "Now how about we get out of here and focus on enjoying each other for a bit."

She smiled at him, his face. His weathered look, the crow's feet and laugh lines, suited him. Gave him a troubadour's energy, marks of a worldly man with plenty of stories to tell. A man who forgave her own marauding. Because he understood, understood her. Related to her. The sort of man she'd searched for before declaring that she was dead inside.

Maybe she could learn to love again, after having forgotten how the magic of romantic abandon felt.

Still cautious, holding back for both their sakes, Megan offered up a lingering, closed-mouth kiss. "Deal."

◊

"You're taking choppy steps. That's why you keep floundering." Megan pulled Thom behind her, the blades of her rented skates scraping the ice. "You have to *glide*."

A few families populated the indoor mall skating rink, too caught up in their own adventures to notice or care about the celebrity in their midst.

"I don't know, sweetheart, gliding might not be in my lexicon of movement." His feet splayed out wide. He flailed his free hand, his grip on her forearm tightening as he groped for balance.

She in turn wobbled, overcorrecting with an arch in her back. The ungainly lurch nearly sent her crashing onto her ass.

"You're going to make me fall," she said through excitable laughter, regaining her stability by pushing him into the clear plastic wall surrounding the rink. Their bodies pressed together, her puffy coat squishing against his bomber jacket. She stole a second to appreciate the whimsy and wholesomeness of the outing. They were bundled up but warm and happy on the inside.

"So keep me steady." His eyes sparkled, his hands roaming down to grab her butt. "Give me something to hold on to."

She rolled her eyes, feeling him harden against her lower belly. "Doesn't work like that. And don't try to distract me. Let's try again. I can't believe how hard you suck at this."

His jaw dropped in an exaggerated, pretend show of outrage. "Some teacher you are."

She smacked the side of his arm. "I never promised a tutorial. You offered the option of mockery yourself."

He huffed, a playful scoff. "I never expected you to seize the opportunity to bully me."

"Okay, fine. One more attempt, then I'm giving up on you as a lost ice skating cause."

He closed his eyes and repeated, "Head in the game, T.J. Head in the game."

With a tug on his hand, she led him back onto the frosty oval. "People call you T.J.?"

Moving beside her, their fingers interlaced, he tilted his lips in a boyish smile, a flutter of shyness totally incongruous with his hotshot, cocky persona. "Not since primary school."

She watched him, intrigued, as they slid a path along the rounded perimeter. Did Thom hesitate to show glimpses of the man behind the mask, the complicated person with layers and dimensions? With pain? Either way, she accepted the honor with pride. "What made you think of that nickname just now?"

He shrugged as they skated in tandem, passing a penalty box occupied by three preteens enraptured by a single cell phone. "I suppose I had a wandering thought about that boy T.J."

"Yeah?" She swerved them with a gentle push to Thom's side, dodging a collision with another couple. "Wanna share?"

"Last time I held hands with a girl in a shopping center was when people called me T.J. I wanted her to like me back so badly. Well, anyway, I had a flashback was all."

The small anecdote nudged her to close some distance between them as they hung a wide turn. She entertained a hazy fantasy of touring with Thom, having fun at concerts, schmoozing at parties. During her adventures in groupiedom, she'd spent plenty of time following bands around. The only difference this time was that she'd be on the arm of a man who cared about her and vice versa. "I do like you back. A lot, actually."

"I just realized something." He lit up in such a charming way that she grinned a truly idiotic grin with a whole lot of teeth.

"Don't keep a girl hanging, T.J."

"We're skating. I'm doing it."

"Holy crap, that's right. Good job. Wow. I wasn't even paying attention."

Newly confident, he slid in front of her and caught her other hand, skating backward and pulling her along for the ride. Where the early bumbling stoked her affection for him, made him more human and real, this show was quietly erotic. Thom's skating prowess was just for her, inspired by her.

"Isn't it incredible how these big moments can sneak up on us when we least expect it?" he said.

How we fall in love when we aren't looking for it?

"Yeah." Weightless and carefree, Megan flew through cool air, her skate blades connecting with gentle scratches as she let go.

They enjoyed each other in silence. After a couple more spins around the track, an unpleasant, burning friction smarted Megan's ankle each time she pushed forward.

"Are you okay? You grimaced." He squeezed her fingers.

"I think I have a blister. Ready to go grab a drink?"

He looked disappointed. "Sure."

She interpreted his tone and body language and made a guess as to what he wanted. "You go around a few more times. Enjoy your new skill. It'll take me a minute to get these off and turn them in."

He dropped a soft, delightfully chilly kiss to her cheek. "Thanks, love. I'll catch up to you in a bit."

"Next stop: Winter Olympics." She released him and skated for the exit. Her bladed boots connected with rubberized flooring, and she hobbled to the benches.

Sure enough, after yanking off her right skate, she spotted

a gnarly red blister. Megan got less than a few seconds to study her wound before the shadow of another person invaded her space bubble. She tensed in the presence of eerie, unsettling energy.

"Where are we?" The voice was female, the question earnest and asked in a normal tone, yet Megan flinched as an uneasy feeling of wrongness took over.

She cut a reluctant glance to the source of the query and had to force herself not to recoil.

Not that anything about the woman looked overtly disconcerting, for other than an albeit odd style, her appearance didn't set off alarm bells.

The stranger was in her thirties, white and of average build and height, with a pretty face. She wore some kind of wrap or turban around her head, the cloth a colorful paisley print, an odd combination with her black t-shirt and matching denim miniskirt. While the headpiece suggested religious devotion, her clothing was anything but conservative. She carried no purse and had no pockets in which to put a phone or keys.

And then there was the matter of her eyes. They were violet. Like, legit purple and obviously color contacts, a showy cosmetic alteration. Yet her startlingly pale face was makeup-free. And she *stared*, wearing this fuzzy expression like she'd just woken up.

"What do you mean, where are we?" Megan shoved out, her brain going numb as she gazed into this person's blinding eyes. They burned, almost, with a cold sort of light.

"Where are we right this minute, in time and space? What is the name of the ground on which we stand?"

"Coral Ridge Mall in Coralville, Iowa." Megan fumbled with her second skate, mentally cursing the stupid shoe when it got stuck. Between the bizarre, antiquated speech and the abnormal questions, this person had her on edge. Was the random lady on drugs?

The hard plastic refused to slide over her foot, and she yanked and snarled until it popped off with a violent pull that knocked her off her equilibrium.

The stranger laughed with a fake, mechanical noise. Her posture was military straight, and her stare was unwavering. Freaking weirdo.

"Can I help you with something?" Megan wrestled into her sneakers, clumsy movements that sent both of her skates tumbling to the padded ground.

She peeked at the ice, where Thom still sailed in big circles, his hands clasped behind his back. Not that she needed him to save her, or needed saving at all. Ugh. Why did this woman give off such yucky vibes? Her energy just felt empty, like a robot's.

Or some other creature lacking a soul. Demons did possess people, but Megan had never seen evidence of this in real life.

"I'm not sure yet." The woman spoke in the wispy monotone of a brainwashed cultist. In a flash, a befuddled expression took over, her unnatural eyes unfocused as she looked around as if lost. "You spoke the code to free me."

Megan's blood turned to ice water. The periphery of her perception blurred, and in one frozen moment she and the odd woman were the only two beings in the mall. Marshalling every ounce of composure, she asked, "What are you?"

The stranger squinted. Blinked. She held out her arm and examined a limb as pallid as a cave dweller's. "An ancient one. Dead, but dreaming. I was decapitated by my slayer, but his blade did not extinguish me."

Megan swore she spied movement under the woman's scarf. A wiggle. Just as she dismissed the notion, a bump pressed into the material, like a hernia popping into sharp relief against skin. The bulge settled and quit squirming.

She looked away as fast as she could, her insides sinking. This wasn't right. Not at all. But she had to get to the bottom of it. "When did I speak a code to free you?"

"MDM. Two-thousand, five-hundred years ago was when I last walked earthly soil." Another disruption writhed under the fabric, prompting the stranger to mutter unintelligible words as she cupped the spot in question. She looked around in furtive, skittish glances, her palm pressed to the side of her head.

Thom skated to the rink's exit, holding the edge as he took careful, clumsy steps down the lone stair connecting the rink to the padded seating area.

Meaning clicked. Roman numerals. Mad Dog Margarita was relevant for the first three letters, what they signified numerically. "What's the significance of you being free? Does the name Mad Dog Margarita mean anything to you?"

Thom clomped over, his strides awkward in the ice skates.

The woman's face twisted into a mask of panic as Thom approached. "I can't kill any more men." She spoke the words with remorse and pathetic helplessness before she ran off clutching her turban.

"What was that about?" As he sat by Megan and pulled off his skates, Thom tracked the fleeing stranger with a turn of his head.

Sprinting with the grace of an athlete, the mystery woman dashed through the automatic exit doors, a parking lot full of cars concealing her until she was gone.

"I don't know. Let's just say something to bring up over at Gary's." She sighed, mulling over the Gary problem. No guarantee anymore that he was an ally or a person who ought to see every single card. "Or not. Maybe we should hold some things back."

"Whatever you think." Being out of the loop on the last encounter, he didn't have much to add. "Can I offer a suggestion?"

She leaned into his side, the frigid, ultraviolet glow of the woman's irises seared onto her brain. "Please."

"Let's go find somewhere that serves hot chocolate with Irish cream liqueur and take a break. A few minutes to ourselves. Then, if we aren't too sloshed or don't end up back in bed, we'll stop by Gary's."

Megan inhaled the leather smell of Thom's jacket, a sweet escape offering a preview of more. "Sounds good."

They would have the rest of the day to investigate, interrogate, and work on the supernatural jigsaw that'd dumped its pieces in her lap beginning with the orphanage incident.

After Thom left, she'd have even more time to poke around by herself. Alone. Again. The inside of her nose stung as they rose together and walked off holding hands, their time together slipping away like sand through a glass aperture. Gary and all the rest would have to wait, because she had the rest of a date to cherish.

Megan banished the blues and asked, "Any more flashbacks to the T.J. years out there?" She pointed to the rink.

He brought her knuckles to his lips and kissed them, chivalrous without being corny as he led her to a bar with a lot of dark woodwork. "Enough about me. Let's get Megan O'Neil's life story. Starting from Megan's earliest memory."

She pretended to cast aspersions on him with her narrow eyes and thinned lips. "You're obsessed with saying my name now, aren't you?"

His face went soft, reverent even, yet with a gleam of rakishness in his eyes that gave his expression an ever-present naughty edge. "I knew yours was worth remembering."

She laughed with affection, at him as well as herself. Maybe she wasn't dead inside, down on love for the rest of her days. Thom James had broken her down, after all, slow and steady with that nonchalant ease of his.

Was long-lasting forever love in their cards? She dared not make a prediction and refused to risk a jinx.

For now, though, walking through a cheesy mall after a productive round of ice skating, Megan had found something beautiful she hadn't known she was looking for. And with as much time as the universe afforded them, she claimed the precious gift as hers.

Because she deserved the little things women like her weren't supposed to get: ice skating, hot chocolate, and holding hands with an awesome man who loved her. As she basked in the joy of those simple pleasures, the dead place inside lit up with the life of a glowing spark. Everything else could wait while she, with Thom's help, nurtured the patient embers of her heart back to good health.

**

Thank you for reading! Did you enjoy? Please add your review because nothing helps an author more and encourages readers to take a chance on a book than a review.

And don't miss more of the *Coven Daughters Origins* coming soon! Until then, discover the book that started it all, HEX, LOVE, AND ROCK & ROLL. Turn the page for a sneak peek!

Also be sure to sign up for the City Owl Press newsletter to receive notice of all book releases!

SNEAK PEEK OF HEX, LOVE, AND ROCK AND ROLL

Helen Schrader hated witches. After all, they'd gotten her thrown into foster care. But as her thirtieth birthday approached, she sat across from a supposed witch named Nerissa and worked up the nerve to ask her for a spell. Funny how the past refused to die.

Pentagram knickknacks and a crystal ball collection decorated the old lady's living room, along with vintage furniture and a framed art print of three women mixing brew in a cauldron. A bookshelf full of texts on witchcraft, world religions, and philosophy completed vivid testimony to authenticity.

People all over Minneapolis swore the crone could conjure fast cash. The pagans who took classes at Helen's yoga studio spoke of Nerissa in the reverent tones of worshipers.

Perhaps the universe began orchestrating the current turn of events when one of Helen's students walked in on her crying over unpaid bills and handed her Nerissa's business card. Unless her visions from years ago kicked some grand plan into motion.

Did everything happen for a reason?

Though the hardened cynic in Helen scoffed at bullshit magical thinking, an atrophied, softer side not yet demolished by life's cruelty yearned to believe in synchronicity and magic.

Sweat glued her jeans to the backs of her thighs as she

adjusted her weight on the sofa cushion. She could stand to do some Zen breathing to calm her nerves. Besides, she'd run out of options to save her business. Her credit was shot, so no more loans. But Light and Enlightened would not become Dark and Forgotten without a final, radical attempt at salvation. Time to take one last shot at rescuing the only permanent home she'd ever known. Throw a Hail Mary pass. She met Nerissa's keen blue eyes and managed a smile.

The universe has a plan. Everything happens for a reason. You've got this.

You are fucking idiot and a loser who is destined to fail.

"You have an impressive book collection." Helen picked a chip in her nail polish as if repetitive motion would banish negative thoughts. "I'm not sure if you got my email about your fee for today. Does twenty dollars work? I'm so sorry I can't offer more."

A lopsided smirk deepened the wrinkles in Nerissa's cheeks. She petted the arm of the leather recliner she sat in and uncrossed her legs beneath a maxi skirt. A knowing tone smoothed the kinks in her low timbre as she said, "Is that why you made an appointment? To discuss literature? Or did you mention the books as a way of confirming my legitimacy?"

Helen drew in a deep inhale and willed the room's sage scent and mellow lighting to relax her before she blundered another attempt at small talk. "Just curious. I've read some of those books. Not the witchy ones, but the Sartre and Nietzsche. 'That which does not kill me makes me stronger' was my motto for awhile. I have an undergrad degree in philosophy. Sorry. I'm rambling."

Yikes, she was a hot and simmering mess. Intelligent aliens were welcome to zap her with a space laser and implant competence into her brain.

Without a word, Nerissa rose. She walked across the living room to the bookcase and ran her finger across spines. "Don't sell yourself short. You have more than an undergrad degree, you started a doctorate. You're smarter than you think, and I can assure you that failure is not in your destiny. Let's have a peek at my favorite book. It's one of the *witchy* ones."

Helen's heart seemed to jump to her throat, and an icy ribbon threaded up her spine. Nerissa must've figured out the facts about her education through research. The other part? Mere coincidence. A nervous laugh bubbled out with her next words. "Is my aura that strong? You practically read my mind."

Nerissa's gray braid swished back and forth as she turned her head over her shoulder. A twinkle in her eye caught slices of afternoon light streaming in through gaps in the drapes.

"There's no *practically* about it. My ability to access your surface thoughts is a sign of our spirit-born connection. I see magic swirled into those beautiful amber irises of yours, too. You are gifted, but we can't step into our deepest truth until we believe in ourselves."

Helen snorted when her stomach went sour. She'd been called a lot of things over the years, but gifted wasn't one of them. Mind reading amounted to an easier sell. This woman was patronizing her due to some ulterior motive. Everybody had one.

"Oh, please. If I was gifted, I'd have more to show for myself by now. Behold, my impressive roster of accomplishments: a pit of debt, a retired stripping career, and a useless degree. Not exactly ticking off boxes on those 'things every woman should have by thirty' checklists."

The self-flagellation lashed Helen to the bone, and her trusty armor of sarcasm didn't protect her from those whip stings. She covered her face and trained her gaze on an area rug, not looking up until the floorboards creaked.

A massive tome in her hands, Nerissa ambled back to her chair and sat. "There will be bigger birthdays if you're lucky. I still remember the sixties. Woodstock. I was the girl in a famous picture, twirling and twirling. I slept with *all* of those rock stars and enjoyed free love."

Heat spread under Helen's breastbone, tightness squeezing her midsection. Was the 'rock stars' comment a sly knock on Helen for falling for the musician ex who cheated on her with every available groupie? A catty little mind-reading trick of Nerissa's?

Whatever. With her life circling the drain, she could not endure head games. Lisa still refused to speak to her. Bad news for a business partner or best friend, let alone both. She had major problems to solve and not a minute to squander.

"Cool. Sounds like fun. I'd like to talk about your services now. My business goes in to foreclosure next week, and my closest friend blames me. I need money. You can do wealth spells, right?"

A grating guffaw rolled out of Nerissa's throat. She opened her volume and leafed. Pages warped from water damage and crowded with words offered coy peeks at possible solutions.

"Patience isn't among your virtues. Hence your tendency to act before thinking and leave projects unfinished. But your drive is noble, and your will is strong. You dare to chase success by any means necessary, which I admire. Takes gumption to sell the spectacle of one's naked flesh to keep the lights on, and don't beat yourself up about the studio. There's a yoga place on every block these days. Lots of entrepreneurial young women such as yourself are losing their shirts teaching Downward Dog."

Helen clamped her teeth down on the tip of her tongue

and swallowed a snarky comeback. Not wise to risk alienating the witch. Better to summon tact and diplomacy.

Nerissa hummed a tune while reading.

Helen tapped her foot. She needed to hit the road before traffic became a zoo, and the final notice of foreclosure stuffed in the bottom of her purse wasn't about to dematerialize.

"Finding any good abundance spells?" The fake-casual lilt in Helen's tone prompted her to roll her eyes at herself. She sucked at tact and diplomacy.

"I want to try an experiment." The gray-haired woman flipped to the front of her book and touched a circle inked on the inside of the cover.

"Alright. Sure." Helen snuck a peek at her watch and squirmed.

"This grimoire was an inheritance from my foremothers. My coven daughter will inherit my sacred text from me to learn the spirit witch's craft and begin the work of the six-fold sisterhood. The spirit element is the most cerebral of the six circles."

God, enough with the pointless anecdotes. Nerissa might have all day to meander, but Helen did not. "Whoever she is will be lucky. Like I said, I'm broke as a joke—"

Another laugh from the old witch made for a jarring interruption. "You may be the *she* in question. Here's a free lesson. Your defeatist tendencies stem from fear of finding your true power, so you self-sabotage in an effort to make yourself less threatening. I understand. We wise women have been taught by the patriarchy to hate our gifts."

Helen ground her molars. Aggravation shot through her in a frying jolt. Cash, not a feminist lecture, would solve her problems. She grabbed her purse off the couch and jumped to her feet. "This was a mistake. I assumed—"

Nerissa muttered in some throaty, incomprehensible

language. The old woman's eyes rolled back in her head. Blank slates of white remained.

Breath vanished from Helen's lungs. The bizarre sight and sounds boggled her imagination until skepticism intervened. Nerissa's eyeball move could be a trick, a result of training ocular muscles.

"A trick? I don't deal in cheap parlor tricks, dear. Now let's see if you are the one."

A pop sounded in Helen's ears. She blinked a few times as a dazed, sleepy sensation disoriented her. Lost to pleasurable mugginess and an odd feeling of time slowing to a crawl, she didn't snap back to lucidity until she noticed the cauldron painting again.

The painting was upside down. No. Correction. *She* was upside down, hanging in midair.

Blood roared in Helen's ears while she scrabbled unsuccessfully to reclaim control of her faculties. A scream tore its way up her throat but somehow died before erupting. Electric with panic, she flailed, spinning in a dizzy circle. A few chaotic seconds later, she recovered some semblance of her bearings and managed to stay still despite waves of queasiness.

The room returned to focus as blurs of color reformed into bookshelves, furniture, and other familiar shapes. *Almost* familiar. Her perception was weird.

Helen gaped when she figured out was was wrong with her surroundings. The furnishings and Nerissa were below her. She was stuck to the damn ceiling. To make matters weirder, another woman now stood in the spot she'd occupied, someone in jeans identical to Helen's.

Shock slammed into her as a realization dawned. She wasn't looking at a third person. She looked down at herself, her own body, while her consciousness floated above. Brunette waves streaked with blonde highlights tumbled over her shoulders. At least she was having a good hair day, because the out-of-body experience blew her mind. Separation from her physical form had been the last thing she'd been expecting during the visit.

A coil of phosphorescent light spiraled upward from the middle of the open book while the witch chanted, "Coven daughter, come to me. Show us truth and clarity."

Discombobulated, Helen squinted against a glare. The beam bent and twisted into a hoop. The space in the middle of the illuminated circle glimmered. Images appeared. A highlight reel of her life played while she gawked.

Nerissa pulled from Helen's memories and projected them at her. *Now* her mind was blown. What else could this be besides hardcore magic?

"I can help you, Helen, but you need to listen. Can you?"

She ought to get in line and embrace the insanity, or she'd soon be begging Dreamgirls to let her hump their germ-infested pole again. Hard pass on the humping. "Yes."

Helen crashed back into her physical form with a boom, knees weak and mind spinning. Reeling from the loss of control, she plopped her butt on the couch and shook herself out of a daze.

"Did your mother and grandmother have the gift?" The witch's eyes returned to normal.

Mother. The sound of the word was profane, like the filthiest curses flung at her.

What should have carried a connotation of loving nurturance dredged up a memory of the time the mother in question shrieked about original sin while she forced Helen to eat the pages of her diary. Recollections of the incident still scraped her raw with phantom pain. She should have learned to stop talking about her visions after that day. Or after the next morning, spent whimpering on the toilet.

"I didn't know my grandmother. My mother had major issues."

"You never had a mother figure who embraced your gift. Tragic." A soft tremble rounded the edges of Nerissa's words. "The visions began at the onset of your menses and lasted for years, didn't they? Trances? Seizures? Mine showed up at menarche and didn't leave until I mastered my craft."

Wow. One other person on the planet could relate to her secret.

"One foster family returned me because my episodes scared their pet rats. Yep. I ranked below rats." She spoke the words in a jesting tone, but the long ago rejection still made Helen's chest ache with old hurt.

"Rats are inherently nervous creatures. Let your pain go and describe the episodes."

"Speaking in tongues, chattering teeth, muscle spasms. Visions of spinning out of my body and flying through the air, seeing women burning at the stake. Wild times. Of course none of my temp families believed me." Helen shrugged, over-affecting nonchalance as the uncomfortable topic poked at her insecurities. Too weird and too spacey. Dissociative. Broken. Bad girl, crazy bitch.

"Flying through the air. Oh, yes. You are spirit born."

For the first time, Helen settled back in her seat, her muscles loosening, curious to know more. "Okay, so I'm spirit born. What should I do to save my studio?"

"You must choose a path to proceed on your actualization."

"Excuse me?"

"To actualize means to coax your abilities to the surface, where you may direct and control them. The power you possess is dormant and churning in your subconscious, so you endured episodes. When witches repress what we do best, we suffer."

Helen put her hands up, palms facing out. She could accept the idea of having some psychic abilities, but being a witch...the notion stretched the limits of plausibility. "Hold up. I don't think I'm a witch."

A shadow passed across Nerissa's eyes. She leaned forward in her chair, close enough for Helen to smell her rosy perfume. "Are you calling me a liar?"

"No. It's difficult to take in, though."

"Why? You came to me for help, and I'm showing you how to get what you want. But if you've changed your mind about needing money, this can end right here." Nerissa closed the book with a definitive snap.

"I'm not quite convinced is all. What's in this for you?"

"When witches practice, our powers enhance each other. Mine will grow in relation to yours. So while I wish to help you because I care about the spiritual health of my coven daughter and want to see the sisterhood come to fruition, I'm also being a teeny bit selfish."

Outlandish, but what if Nerissa was right? God, the possibilities for turning her life around. She hadn't taken a chance coming to the witch's home only to run out when things got strange. No more quitting, no more failure. Time to nut up or shut up.

"Fine. I'm all in. You were saying. Initiation. Spirit element. Smash the patriarchy with our broomsticks. How do I choose a path?"

"Your choices are Right Hand or Left Hand path. The Right Hand path draws from your internal strengths and abilities, in your case latent color magic. Astral projection and remote viewing would also come from marshalling the Right."

"How does color magic work?"

"The expression is unique to the witch. You'd call out to

meaningful colors in your life and weave emotional union with them to perform spells."

"Such as visualizing the color green for money."

Nerissa shrugged. "If you're thinking long-term, sure."

The words "long-term" bounced around in a series of bothersome echoes. Long-term might not suffice. "What's up with the Left?"

"Left Hand powers originate from outside. Think transferring energy into objects in order to manipulate them, or splitting your psyche so as to exist in two places at once. The Left is potent and capable of producing immediate results, but also volatile and dark."

A surge of curiosity charged through Helen. She scooted to the edge of her seat. Potent power and speedy results could save L&E before the bank snatched it away and Helen and Lisa trudged out carrying boxes.

Helen had slunk out of many front doors with tears in her eyes. Never again.

She pursed her lips, though, wavering at what volatile and dark might mean. In all likelihood, something bad. Yet depending on inner strengths didn't seem like the right move, not when one of Helen's dumb mistakes all but catapulted the studio into the abyss.

"Have you chosen?" Nerissa drummed her fingers on the book's cover.

Bottom line, she could not afford to wait. "I choose the Left Hand path."

"There will be a cost." Nerissa rose and offered Helen the grimoire.

"What is it?" Helen accepted, her arms straining under the book's weight.

Nerissa walked to a credenza. Jars filled with liquids in a variety of colors cluttered the top. Helen watched with interest as the old lady rummaged in a drawer.

The elder witch returned with a small sack made of black velvet and a jar half full of clear fluid. She handed over the pouch. "Depends on one's constitution. Could be as trivial as a stomachache."

Helen took the bag, taking a moment to stroke the silky material. She loosened a string and peered in. Crystals in a rainbow of colors sparkled one after the other as if they communicated. "But it could be worse."

"Oh, yes."

"What's the worst case scenario?"

"If the universe decides the darkness wasn't yours to take, it might generate a hex as punishment for selecting the wrong magic. Think karma, but magnified tenfold."

Helen's insides dropped. "Hold up. I don't need more trouble. How would I deal with a hex?"

"Read your book. That's the answer to all of your questions. But first, deploy the crystals. They are sentient and absorbent, and the clear ones are the most pliable and receptive to their witch's will. Give both clear stones away to good people before you undertake your study, as cultivating others' energies will refine your powers. Make sure to set a mental intention before gifting this pair of crystals. Done correctly, this means giving each one precise directions. Otherwise, the hex might begin with dark entities latching on to one or both stones. Once demons establish communion, they can possess crystals."

Yawning, Nerissa thrust the jar at Helen. "Drink this and leave. The Reveal spell I did drained my energy. If I don't get my nap in, my weakened state could compromise you."

Though her pulse accelerated, Helen took the container and unscrewed its lid. She chugged, gag reflex lurching as she downed the sour glop. Her eyes watered, and nausea roiled her insides, but she finished the nasty potion. Go big or go home. "So twenty bucks is okay?"

"We'll settle up down the road." The old woman's eyelids fluttered closed as she sagged in her chair. "Study now."

A rush of pride prompted Helen to straighten her spine. She could be a decent student. Armed with a big book of witchiness and the crystals, she placed her empty jar on a coffee table and sauntered to the front door of the bungalow with her head held high.

The plan: give away two crystals, figure out magic, get L&E solvent, and save her dearest friendship. Doable? Helen smiled and hugged the grimoire to her chest. Hell yeah.

"*Sacrificium.*" A calm, male voice spoke inside of Helen's head. An itchy surge of adrenaline shot to her toes. Though she'd never taken Latin, she sure got the gist—sacrifice.

Her hand tensed on the doorknob, and she glanced at Nerissa. "Did you hear that?"

"No!" Nerissa bolted upright. Her mouth dropped, and her eyes stretched wide, but the show of fear in her expression fled as fast as it came.

Helen's mouth dried. Talk about a bad omen double whammy. "Are you okay?"

Rubbing her temples, the elder looked around the room. "I'm fine. Take care."

Helen jetted to her Mini Cooper. As she fumbled for her keys, a plume of milky smoke erupted in the recesses of her consciousness, vanishing a second after it arrived. She tried to disregard the inexplicable intrusion. Probably just her magic settling in.

She drove to the Minnesota State Fair, but by the time she squeezed between two cars in a dusty makeshift lot, she hadn't managed to forget the creepy voice and smoke.

A definitive slam of her door shoved the unsettling events out of her mind, and she strode to the flapping banner marking the entrance to the fairgrounds.

Today belonged in the win column, damn it.

◊

Don't stop now. Keep reading with your copy of HEX, LOVE, AND ROCK & ROLL available now.

Don't miss more of the Coven Daughters Origins coming soon, and find more from Kat Turner at katturnerauthor.com

Until then, discover the book that started it all, HEX, LOVE, AND ROCK & ROLL

◊

With a business skidding toward bankruptcy and bone-dry bank account, Helen Schrader is willing to do the unthinkable. But what will happen when she hires a witch to cast a money spell?

When the spell sets in motion her own latent magic and her inexperience causes her to accidentally hex her celebrity crush, rocker Brian Shepherd, all that good fortune she hoped for flies out of the window.

Now, Helen and Brian struggle to break the curse and tackle their growing feelings for each other. Problem is, the harder they fall for each other, the deadlier the curse becomes.

But as a dark magic cult with an unquenchable thirst for power closes in on them, the couple will have to face more than just their inconvenient desire. With time running out and danger mounting, can they beat the hex before Brian becomes its next victim?

◊

Please sign up for the City Owl Press newsletter for chances to win special subscriber-only contests and giveaways as well as receiving information on upcoming releases and special excerpts.

All reviews are **welcome** and **appreciated**. Please consider leaving one on your favorite social media and book buying sites.

For books in the world of romance and speculative fiction that embody Innovation, Creativity, and Affordability, check out City Owl Press at www.cityowlpress.com.

ACKNOWLEDGMENTS

Thank you to everyone who has bought, read, reviewed, boosted, hyped, and otherwise supported my stories. Your encouragement is my fuel to keep writing, and I appreciate each one of you more than you will ever know. May you love Thom and Megan as much as I do. This couple holds a special place in my heart, and it is truly my pleasure to share them with you.

ABOUT THE AUTHOR

 KAT TURNER is an award-winning author of paranormal romance and urban fantasy as well as the occasional thriller. Her favorite stories to write are those that combine action and adventure with magic, dry humor, and steamy romance if the situation allows. She lives is Kentucky with her family, where she can mostly be found practicing yoga, taking nature walks, or getting lost in the corridors of her own imagination. Kat loves to connect with readers, so don't be shy about getting in touch!

linktr.ee/katturnerauthor

ABOUT THE PUBLISHER

City Owl Press is a cutting edge indie publishing company, bringing the world of romance and speculative fiction to discerning readers.

Escape Your World. Get Lost in Ours!

www.cityowlpress.com

facebook.com/YourCityOwlPress
twitter.com/cityowlpress
instagram.com/cityowlbooks
pinterest.com/cityowlpress